TELL ME YOU WANT ME

A novel by

Amelia James

TELL ME YOU WANT ME

THIRD EDITION SOFTCOVER
ISBN: 1622538080
ISBN-13: 978-1-62253-808-9

Edited by Stevie Mikayne and Lane Diamond

Printed in the U.S.A.

www.EvolvedPub.com
Evolved Publishing LLC
Cartersville, Georgia

Printed in Book Antiqua font.

DEDICATION:

For my mother-in-law,
who has provided unending support and encouragement.

Prologue

"They're fighting again." Charles Austin Sinclair III looked up from his Nintendo football game toward his bedroom door. His parents' angry voices reached him even though his solid oak door was closed.

"Did she find out about another girlfriend?" Jack Wheeler moved his players into position. One more touchdown would put him in the lead.

Austin saw Jack roll his eyes right before he snapped the ball. If they stopped what they were doing every time Austin's parents argued, they would never get anything done. Jack was Austin's best friend since forever—well, since the third grade—but that was forever to the ten-year-olds.

"Yeah," Austin said, "that's what they always fight about. Girls are trouble."

"They sure like you, though."

"Ugh."

The girls in their class often giggled and whispered things like 'so cute' and 'dreamy' when Austin was around. He would scrunch up his face and stick out his tongue in response. Annoying girls.

His parents argued in the hallway now, just a few feet from his room. He picked up the remote and turned up the volume, but it didn't help.

His defensive line jumped on Jack's receiver. "Fourth down. You gotta settle for a field goal."

"You wish." Jack faked the field goal and threw a pass to the end zone. "Touchdown!"

Austin groaned and dropped his controller in his lap. Angry voices from the hall turned his attention to the door again, and he let out a huge sigh.

"At least your dad doesn't hit your mom," Jack said, lining up for the extra point.

"Yeah, this fight will be over pretty soon."

"I've had enough, Charles," his mother yelled. "I won't forgive you this time."

Austin rolled his eyes and dramatized his father's next words.

"I won't do it again, Emma. I promise."

Jack clapped a hand over his mouth but couldn't keep the laughter from his eyes as Austin offered the perfect exaggeration of his father, his big blue eyes somehow pleading innocence and begging forgiveness at the same time.

"That's what you said the last...." She paused.

Austin held up three fingers—nope—four.

"...the last four times I caught you."

"Those women meant nothing to me. They were just... entertainment. As soon as I get bored with one, I move on to another. You know that."

"That's supposed to make me feel better?"

"I can fix this. Give me another chance."

Austin clasped his hands together and fell to his knees.

Jack grabbed a pillow and smothered his giggles.

"No more second chances," Austin's mother said in an oddly calm tone.

Austin stood up and mimicked his mother's scowl, waiting for her next line.

"I want a divorce, Charles."

Wait. She wasn't supposed to say that. She was supposed to make him promise never to do it again. Austin's lip quivered and tears pricked his eyes. Even Jack looked sober.

"No. Emma, I love you."

Austin blinked back tears as his mother sobbed. He went to the door and leaned in, pressing his ear against it.

"How can you say that after everything you've done to me? Do you really expect me to believe you?"

Austin heard her run down the hall and slam the door; then he heard his father stomp out to the garage and drive away.

His knees buckled under him and he plopped hard onto the floor. "It's not supposed to end like that."

Jack sat beside him, all humor gone from his face.

"She's supposed to come in and tell me everything's going to be all right. He's supposed to promise he'll never hurt her again. He's not supposed to leave."

Jack shuddered. "Maybe he'll come back. My dad always came back."

"What if he doesn't?"

***

His mom came in much later, when Austin was supposed to be asleep. She sat down on the edge of his bed and ran her fingers through his hair. "Oh, Austin, you are my heart."

He kept his eyes closed. Jack lay in the top bunk, silent and still.

"You're so much like your father it scares me." She leaned over and kissed his forehead. "Please don't be like him. Don't hurt a woman you love." She sobbed quietly. "Don't make her cry."

She got up and left, never seeing the tear trickling down Austin's cheek.

He wished he *was* asleep, that he would wake up in the bright sunshine and find out he'd suffered a bad dream. Yet when he opened his eyes, the darkness remained. So very dark.

"Did you hear that?" He knew Jack was listening. Best friends always listened.

"Yeah, I heard." Jack looked down over the edge of the bunk. "What are you going to do?"

"I don't know." He loved his mother, and didn't want her to hurt anymore. He didn't want her to cry.

"I've never seen your mom cry like that before."

Austin wiped his tears away, forgetting Jack couldn't see him in the dark. "I have. Every time he—" The words stuck in his throat and his voice broke.

Jack's voice echoed the pain in Austin's heart. "Maybe it'll be better if they get divorced. Maybe they'll stop fighting."

"Do you think so?"

"I don't know. I hope so."

Austin sniffled and pulled the blankets up to his chin. "They're supposed to love each other." He curled up in the blankets and tried to get warm. "Dad told Mom he loved her, but she didn't believe him. She still wants a divorce."

"My dad said he loved my mom too, but he still hurt her."

"See? Love hurts. Love makes you hurt people and you get hurt too." His heart turned as cold and dark as the emptiness surrounding him. "I'm never going to fall in love."

Chapter 1

"Hey, Jane! Heads up!"

Jane Elliot was not easily distracted, so when Ryan called her name, she ignored him. Focused, she dribbled the soccer ball down the field. Brenda set up to defend the goal, but she was just a minor obstacle. Jane gave the goalie her most intimidating snarl, and laughed when Brenda actually took a step back.

"Jane, duck!" Brenda yelled.

Duck? Why?

The back of Jane's head exploded and stars spun around her eyes. She dropped to her knees and grabbed her throbbing skull. From the corner of her swirling eyes, she saw Ryan and Brenda running to help.

"Sorry." Ryan took her arm and helped her up. "That one got away from me."

When Jane's eyes finally uncrossed, she noticed a football wobbling at her feet. She picked it up and threw it back to Ryan. "Keep your ball on your side of the field," she grumbled, relieved she could put a coherent sentence together.

"How's your head?" Ryan walked her to the bleachers and made her sit down.

"Still attached, lucky for you."

"I tried to warn you."

"I know, but once I set my mind on something, I won't give up."

"I noticed."

She sipped the water Ryan gave her, breathed deep in between sips, and waited for the soccer field to stop spinning. Coach checked her eyes for a concussion, but he didn't see any serious damage, so he ended practice for the day.

Jane stayed at the soccer field, kicking goals to make up for the one she'd missed. It was Ryan's fault she'd missed it, but scoring points, even if just in practice, always made her feel better.

Burnt orange clouds streaked across the twilight blue sky as the sun set over the Bayfield College athletic fields. Fall in the Midwest brought short days and cold nights—and the beginning of Jane's senior year. She looked forward to finishing school and moving on to the next phase of her life— the next step toward her career goal.

She picked up her duffle bag and jogged back to the gym. Inside it was warm and peaceful, but not as quiet as she'd expected it to be.

"Oh, oh please...."

The strange voice hit her as soon as she entered the women's locker room, which should have been empty by now. The female voice, gasping and begging, came from the shower. Was someone hurt?

"Oh God...."

Jane turned the corner into the shower area and stopped short.

A girl leaned against the tile wall—not exactly begging for help. She was bent forward, her short skirt held above her waist by the young man behind her.

"Mmm... that's it, baby," she groaned. "You know what I like."

No, the girl wasn't begging for help; she was begging for more.

Jane didn't recognize the girl—all the cheerleaders looked the same to her—but there was no mistaking the ass behind her: Austin Sinclair, starting quarterback, campus heartbreaker.

His thick chocolate-brown hair stood out in all directions, as if the girl had been running her hands through it, but then it always looked like that. Tall and strong, with a smile like an angel, and deep blue eyes that promised sin, Austin could have had any girl he wanted. And he did. His devilish good looks got the girls' attention, and his boyish charm, infectious laugh and—according to the school gossip—his talent in bed, kept them coming back for more. Actually, the stories said his sexual escapades went far beyond the bedroom, so Jane wasn't surprised to find him here.

She rolled her eyes. Why did she have to stumble across his latest adventure?

She intentionally slammed her duffle bag into the nearest locker. "Oops."

The girl shrieked and covered herself, but Austin pulled the irritated cheerleader close and whispered something in her ear that made her glare at Jane. He kissed her cheek and sent her to get dressed. Then he winked at Jane and flashed that infamous smile. "Did you like that, sweetheart? Wanna be next?"

"*Your* next? Keep dreaming." She rolled her eyes again, and walked to her locker, ignoring the furious cheerleader scurrying from the room.

The bad boy strolled out of the shower, zipping up his jeans. He leaned against a row of lockers and folded his arms over his chest, watching her put away her soccer gear.

Jane shivered as his gaze roamed over her body like a pair of exploring hands, touching and lingering in places no other man had noticed before.

"Mm-mm, you're just the kind of girl a man likes to dream about."

Oh my God, did he really just say that? About me? She couldn't look at him. He flirted with every girl on campus, so she knew it didn't mean anything. Still, he was flirting with *her*. Guys didn't flirt with her often—or at all. Not that it mattered. Pursuing her career was more important than flirting with guys.

She packed her bag and dug through her locker as if he didn't exist.

Austin ran his fingers through his wild hair and shifted his weight. His jaw tightened for a moment, but then that naughty smile returned. "I'll forgive you for interrupting if you promise not to tell the dean I was in here."

Jane laughed. "I won't have to tell. Everyone knows you're no stranger to the girls' locker room." Even Sara, her best friend and least athletic person on the planet, had told stories about Austin's favorite playing field.

"Ouch baby."

"Don't call me baby."

"Sorry, sweetheart." He grinned at her.

"I have a name!" She slammed the locker shut and glared back.

"I know you do." The grin started to fade and he shifted again.

"This school isn't that big. I know your name, Charles Austin Sinclair III." She smiled as that charming grin turned into an angry scowl.

"Don't call me that. Ever." He ground the words out through clenched teeth.

"Surely you must know my name."

"You bet I do." He paused, his eyes rolling to the right, searching his memory. "I'm just playing with you." The grin returned. "Or I'd like to."

She saw right through his little game. Well, she could play too. Obviously, he knew nothing about her, so she might as well have some fun with him. "You're not the only one...."

Actually, he was. Jane's mother hadn't let her date in high school, and the trend had continued right into college. *Focus on your studies, Jane*, her mother had told her. *Don't let boys distract you.*

"Oh yeah?" Austin's eyes lit up and Jane wondered what had sparked his interest. He moved closer to her. "Where do I get in line?"

She wanted to tell him to get behind her, but she'd just witnessed what he could do to a girl from behind. Might not be such a bad thing.

The cheerleader had seemed to enjoy it. Jane wondered what it would feel like to let him touch her. She stole a glance at his hands. Such long fingers.... A little shiver ran down her spine and she bit her lip before she said anything stupid.

"Come on, sugar–"

"What's my name?"

"Um... Jenna."

"Wrong answer."

"Jenny."

"Keep trying." If he stuck with J names, he might stumble onto it.

"I will." He settled back against the locker next to her as if he belonged there. "Come have a drink with me and I'll figure it out."

I should say no. "Isn't there a frustrated cheerleader you should be consoling?"

He chuckled. "Probably. She'll wait."

Jane had no doubt she would. "I need to study." School was more important than Austin Sinclair—or any other man.

"So do I, but I don't want to." He moved closer to her and brushed her hair back over her shoulder, caressing her skin. "I want to be with you."

His light, provocative touch dared her to ask for more. If his fingers felt that good in her hair, what would his hands feel like on her body? She stepped back, unwilling to allow those thoughts. "Do you always get what you want?"

"Yep."

Just a hint of a smile touched his lips, but his eyes—*oooh, his eyes*—promised she would get everything she wanted too. What did she want that he could give her? A little freedom, a little fun, and a lot of trouble. *Dangerous thoughts about a dangerous man.* Jane almost smiled in return. Did she really want that? She shook her head. "Why me?"

"Why not? You're very pretty, and I can tell you need to have a little fun."

Fun. That might be enough for him, but not for her. She refused to be just another notch on his bedpost.

"I have other plans." She swung her heavy backpack over her shoulder and wobbled backwards when the books shifted, nearly knocking her to the floor. She had goals to accomplish, dreams to reach for. Fun played no part in her plans.

"Not anymore."

"Wow, that's overconfident."

"Come on, baby. Are you up for it?"

She ignored that challenge and shot back one of her own. "Say my name."

"What's the matter... Gina?"

"Wrong again."

"I'm really bad at names."

He probably rarely made the effort to remember them, not when *baby* or *sweetheart* would do. "I noticed, but I hear you're good at everything else." *Did I say that out loud?*

Austin laughed. "That's true. I may not remember your name, but I will remember what you like in bed, where you like to be touched, how you like to be kissed... and where." His voice got soft and husky as he backed her up against the lockers, his body almost touching hers, his lips close but still so far away. "Come with me, and I'll give you something to remember."

A little thrill shot through her body, and for a moment Jane debated tossing her books on the floor and grabbing the fun he promised. Austin pursued pleasure without reservation, without hesitation, and apparently, without rules. How else could he go from screwing a bouncy blonde cheerleader to seducing boring bookworm Jane in the space of a few minutes?

"No." There. She finally said it.

"I'm sorry, what did you say?" He leaned back to look at her.

She couldn't help but laugh. "I figured you wouldn't understand that word." She pushed him away.

He stood with his hands on his hips, his eyes intent on her. "Oh, I understand plenty. You think you can resist me."

"Yes, I can." *But do I want to?*

"You think you're immune to my charms."

"I am." *For now.*

A slow, practiced smile curved his lips, and something dangerous danced in his eyes. "We'll see how long that lasts."

She had a feeling it wouldn't last long at all. "Are we done now?" She held her bag tighter and headed for the door.

He followed her. "Not by a long shot, darlin'."

She stopped and fixed her eyes on him.

"Julia."

"Still wrong." When she reached the locker room door, he held it open for her. Nice move, but she could practically see his ulterior motive taunting her in his eyes.

"The next time we meet, I won't be so nice." Austin winked at her and disappeared down the hallway.

Jane leaned back against the wall and caught her breath. *Darn it.* She'd said *no.* No next time. *So why am I thinking about a next time?*

***

Austin jumped in his Jeep and drove home , still thinking about the girl he'd met in the locker room—not the cheerleader, but the soccer babe. He couldn't believe she'd said no to an innocent drink. Okay—not so innocent. Dirty thoughts had run through his calculating mind. A drink might have loosened her up a little and then.... He didn't hear "no" often, if at all. Still, he was no quitter. He wouldn't take no for an answer until she said it, and meant it.

He opened the door to his apartment, and a football bounced off his head. "What the hell?"

"That's why you're a quarterback instead of a receiver." Jack Wheeler laughed.

"Remind me to trade you in for a prettier roommate," Austin grumbled, his head throbbing. "One who doesn't throw like a girl."

"Carrie was looking for you. Man, was she ever pissed." Jack tossed the football into his bedroom and sat down on the couch. "What did you do to her?"

Austin dropped his backpack on the coffee table and sat down in the recliner next to the couch. He remembered doing some very interesting things to Carrie, but nothing that would— "Oh yeah." He chuckled. "We kinda got interrupted."

"Busted again? You're gonna get kicked out of school if you're not careful."

"Nah. Dean Francis will never boot me." Austin had a lot of practice talking himself out of trouble.

"Yeah, you're lucky the dean is an *understanding* woman."

"Luck has nothing to do with it."

"So who caught you this time?"

"Another girl."

"Oh man, no wonder Carrie was so mad. Did one of your exes catch you?"

"Nope. I've never met this girl before. I've seen her around, but for the life of me, I can't remember her name."

"I'm not surprised. What does she look like?"

She looked a little bit like... someone else. *She'd* worn glasses too. *Damn it, why did I have to remember that?* "Pretty brunette, green eyes. She wears those sexy librarian glasses."

The soccer babe had looked familiar, but he'd never notice her in a crowd. She blended in and disappeared, but now that Austin had taken a good look at her, he'd noticed a beauty he'd never seen before. She hadn't worn her glasses at practice, so he'd admired her gorgeous green eyes. The rich brown hair she usually kept pinned up flowed over her shoulders, curling a bit where sweat made it damp.

Jack nodded. "Nice."

She had a toned and athletic body—the kind made for *full contact* sports. "Not a lot of curves, but she looks like the type who has stamina. I'll bet she could keep up with me in bed." That thought raised him to full attention. Natalie was slender and delicate. The soccer babe could easily kick her ass.

"I'll bet you'd like to find out."

"Oh yeah. Sweet apple-sized breasts with fat nipples I could see under her shirt." Natalie had grapefruit-sized.... *Stop comparing!*

Jack laughed. "Okay, you noticed her body. So what's she like?"

"Stubborn. She refused to go out with me, and she wouldn't tell me her name."

"Did you ask her?"

"Uh...." Austin relived their conversation in his head. "No, I didn't think of that."

"Dumbass. You'd have forgotten it by now, anyway."

"Probably. Too many women in my life. I get them all confused." Not that he complained. He knew all the in-demand girls, the easy girls, and the girls who played hard to get.

But he didn't know *her*.

"Wait... you asked her out and she said no?"

"Yeah. Surprised me too, but she'll have a different answer next time."

"It might help if you knew her name. Some girls like that."

"It might help if you weren't such a smartass. She plays soccer. Any idea who she is?"

Jack smiled and his eyes danced. "Nope."

"Damn it." Austin jumped off the couch and wrenched open the fridge. He grabbed a beer and popped the top off, hoping it would wash away the sudden flood of bad memories swirling around him. "She reminds me of Nat."

Jack raised an eyebrow and joined him in the kitchen. "How?"

"They're the same type: book nerd, top of the honor roll, math club president or some bullshit like that."

"How do you know your soccer girl was president of the math club?"

"I don't." He snarled and polished off his beer, slapping the empty bottle on the table. "She has that look... like a dumb jock isn't good enough for her."

"She's a jock too."

Austin snorted. "I swore I'd never fall for a girl again. I can't."

"So she looks like Nat?"

Austin shook his head. "Not exactly like her. Just the glasses." He searched the fridge for another beer, but the case was empty.

"That doesn't mean she's gonna...." Jack put a hand on his friend's shoulder. "She's not gonna do what Nat did to you."

The one time he'd ignored his father's advice; the one time he decided to take a risk and give his heart to a girl, she'd rejected him. "Damn right. I will not fall for this girl. Keepin' it casual. Just fun. No promises."

"There ya go." Jack grinned. "What are you gonna do about Carrie?"

"Huh? Oh yeah. Carrie." He'd already decided to be done with Carrie. "I'll make it up to her." *Okay, not quite done.*

"And then?"

"Then I'll find out who this soccer babe is and make her say yes." *Over and over.*

Jack shook his head. "I've known you since the third grade, and I can't think of a single girl who's said no to you and meant it."

Austin smiled. "She will not be the first."

"Wanna bet on it?"

"Loser buys me a six-pack."

"Loser buys *me* a case of Coke."

"Nope." Austin smiled. "I will not lose."

Chapter 2

Ugh. Why can't I get him out of my head? Jane shoved the refrigerator door shut and tossed the mushrooms on the counter next to the green pepper. A twisted thought tickled her brain as she picked up the knife... but no, she didn't want to hurt Austin. She inspected the knife, catching her reflection in the shiny blade. Frustration, excitement, nervousness—but no anger—showed on her face. Something else too. *Aroused? What does that look like?*

Jane chopped the mushrooms like a skilled chef. Cooking was her favorite escape. When she created a recipe, everything else melted away—the pressures of school, her mother's strict rules, and a yummy young man who had no business interrupting her life to begin with.

Why did she find him so appealing? He was not the kind of man she normally looked for. Okay, she hadn't been looking, but if she decided to, she definitely wouldn't want a guy who loved sex, loved pleasure, loved freedom....

Actually, that did sound pretty appealing.

Cooking may have given her the escape she craved, but real freedom eluded her. She'd left her mother's house, but still wrestled with the guilt her mother had heaped on her all her life. Did she feel guilty for wanting Austin? Jane smiled. Her mother definitely would not approve.

No, she couldn't go out with Austin just to spite her mother. In fact, she'd never tell her. Still, the idea of going out with him lingered and nagged at her. He would be a good time, for sure. Everyone on campus knew that. He was the perfect guy just to have fun with, because he wouldn't stick around—a minor diversion, not a major distraction.

But it would be wrong to treat Austin that way. She couldn't play the way he did.

On the other hand... he would be a lot of fun to fool around with, and as he'd pointed out, she needed to have a little fun. A tiny shiver ran down her spine at the thought of the kind of fun she could have with that man.

Stop it, stop it, stop it! Do not think about him anymore! Where is that green pepper? Jane stabbed it with the butcher knife and dropped it on the cutting board.

The front door opened and closed, and she knew without looking that her roommate, Sara Jensen, was home.

"Mmm... what's for dinner?"

Jane so focused on the green pepper she was chopping that she didn't fully register Sara's question—like the vague aftereffect of a dream.

"Hey Jane...."

The knife flew out of Jane's hand and landed in the sink. "Oh, it's you."

"What are you making?" Sara stepped back, away from the knives.

"Huh? Oh, just something I threw together."

Sara stood over the stove and inhaled while Jane stirred chicken, mushrooms, and olives in a thick, bubbling sauce. "I wish I could just throw something together like you do."

Jane tossed the peppers in the sauce and tasted it. Did she need to add garlic or shallots? She'd made this sauce a hundred times. Why couldn't she remember it?

"Taste this. Something's missing." She held up a spoonful.

"Mmm...." Sara licked her lips. "Don't you put basil in this?"

"Basil. That's it." She stirred in a pinch of the pungent herb. "Nope, still not right."

"What's the matter with you?"

She would not start thinking about him again. "Nothing." She wouldn't think about that devilish smile, those dangerous eyes....

Sara smiled. "*Nothing* makes you blush?"

"Hot stove."

"Yeah right." Sara leaned against the counter. "You met a guy."

The spoon in her hand hit the stove. "How did you know?"

"I didn't." Sara grinned and sat down at the table. "Tell me everything. Is he cute? Is he nice? Does he like you? Did he ask you out?"

Jane laughed. "One question at a time. Yes, he's very cute." *More like sinfully delicious—yeah that's it. Oh, good Lord, Jane! Food and sex? I need to have a lot of fun.*

"So how did you meet him?"

She decided not to tell Sara that story. "Um... I saw him at the gym. He's a football player."

"Mmm... I don't like football, but I like football players." Sara's eyes sparkled. "Is he interested in you or is this a one-sided crush?"

"Oh, he's interested."

Austin had made no effort to hide his desire. Jane, on the other hand, nearly chopped off her fingers trying to figure out what she wanted.

"What's his major? Is he a senior too?"

"I don't know. We didn't talk about that."

Sara looked unusually excited about this. "What did you talk about?"

"Nothing important." Just her name. "He flirted with me a lot."

"Flirting is good, especially when it's directed at you. Did he ask you out?"

"Yes."

"And? Don't keep me in suspense!" Sara practically bounced off the chair.

"And I said no." *Is that regret I'm feeling?*

"Why? You need to get out and have some fun. When was the last time you had a date?"

"It's been a while."

"I don't think you've been out with a guy since last year. You shouldn't be turning down dates. It's not like you get a lot of offers."

"Thanks for reminding me."

"Sorry. I just meant you need to take advantage of your opportunities."

"I'm not really interested in dating right now. This is my senior year of college, and it's going to be tough. I need to focus on school." That came out like a rehearsed excuse.

"I know, believe me, but you need to take a break once in a while and just have a good time."

Austin could definitely show a girl a good time. She needed a break, and he would only be a temporary distraction—and a fun one.

Jane could think of a lot of reasons why she should, and only one reason why she shouldn't. "He's not the right guy."

"He doesn't have to be the 'right' guy. Just enjoy it and see what happens." Sara grinned.

"Maybe." *Take the risk. Enjoy it while it lasts.*

"No maybes. I hate maybes. If he's a nice guy, give him a chance."

Jane shivered when she remembered Austin's parting words. "He's not a nice guy."

She suddenly realized that was why she liked him. Austin was a bad boy, and that bad boy brought out the bad girl inside her—way deep down inside her.

"What does that mean?"

"He's Austin Sinclair."

Sara's excited smile disappeared. "Are you serious?"

"Yeah."

"Ugh. Forget everything I just said. Austin is not the guy you take a chance with."

Oh, but Jane wanted to. If they met again—or *when*, if Austin had his way—she wouldn't be able to say no and mean it. "It could be fun."

"No. He's not worth the trouble. Trust me." Sara looked at the stove and her stomach growled. "I'm not hungry." She went to her room and shut the door.

Jane's wonderful sauce splattered all over the stove, but she hardly noticed. As soon as she'd said Austin Sinclair, Sara had gone from an enthusiastic supporter to a doomsday prophet.

What does she know that I don't?

***

For the first time in three years, Austin noticed the soccer field located right next to the football field. Silver metal soccer bleachers, placed back-to-back with the solid wood football grandstands, separated the two fields.

He searched the soccer field for the girl he'd met in the locker room yesterday, and when he found her, he immediately started staring. Watching her fight off one defender after another, sprinting down the field toward the goal, took his breath away. The girl looked tough and fast, something he admired and respected. Why hadn't he ever noticed her before? He knew her name. He had to know her name. *What is it?*

As he stared across the empty field, searching his brain for the elusive name, another memory accosted him. He'd met Nat on a football field in high school. She'd stood on the sideline, screaming and cheering with everyone else after he'd won the first of three state championships. Maybe the excitement of the unexpected comeback had drawn them together. But it couldn't keep them together.

Walk it off, man. Austin paced beside the stands, testing his strength and riding out the pain until his determination returned. Soccer babe would fall for *him*—not the other way around.

He waited for her in the gap between the grandstands and the bleachers, whistling at her when she walked by. "Hey baby!"

She looked up and smiled, but when he whistled again, she scowled and kept walking. "Don't expect me to come running like a lovesick puppy."

He hadn't meant to summon her like a dog. He ran after her. "I was just trying to get your attention."

"Have you figured out my name yet?"

Shit. He'd hoped he could avoid that a while longer. "Jenny."

"You already tried that one."

"Damn it."

She choked back a laugh. "If you won't bother to try, then I won't bother with you."

Ouch. She had him there. Austin turned on the charm, knowing he could talk himself out of this. "You have me so hot and bothered, I can't think straight."

This time she did laugh. "Do girls really fall for that?"

Damn it! His flirting skill had never failed him before. "Yeah, they do. It's amazing how far a little bit of truth and a lot of charm will get me."

She stopped and looked at him. "So where's the truth?" Her eyes had softened a bit, and she'd lost the sarcastic tone.

Austin stepped close and slid his hands in her hair, looking straight into those doubting green eyes. He abandoned his smooth words and clever lines, and let her see a flash of honesty. "I am very attracted to you."

She smiled at him, her resistance starting to crumble. "I thought it was the 'I can't think straight' part."

He grinned. "Mm... my girl likes to tease."

"Your girl?" Her mouth fell open.

He laughed as she did her best to look shocked and offended. Girls claimed they didn't like possessive guys, but in his experience they really did, especially when he was the guy. Some of the tension left her body. Maybe that stubborn wall had started to crack.

He chipped away at it. "You like me. Come on, admit it."

"I do not."

"Yes you do. I can tell."

"How?" She trembled.

"You haven't stopped smiling since I said I was attracted to you—"

Her lips formed a hard line.

"—and you're still letting me touch you."

She gasped and stepped back.

He laughed. "Give in, sweetheart. Tell me you want me."

"No way."

He'd had a lot of practice reading women, and could spot faked denial every time. Her lips said no, but her hot pink cheeks and sparkling emerald eyes said yes. She wanted him. Only a matter of time until she admitted it.

He shrugged his shoulders. "Okay, I can be patient."

"That's not what I heard."

"You know more about me than I know about you. That's hardly fair."

She raised her chin and looked down her nose at him. "You know how to fix that."

"Yes I do." He pulled her close, his gaze on her full red lips.

She tried to push him back. "That's not what I meant."

"Come have a drink with me, and we'll get to know each other real well." The smile he gave her made most women melt in his arms.

"No."

Holy hell, she's stubborn. "All right, skip the drinks. Just come to bed with me."

"No. If I go out with you, it's going to be a real date—dinner, movie... the works. You are going to treat me like a queen."

Austin just couldn't close his mouth fast enough. "And then I'll take you to bed and treat you like the castle whore." *Damn it, I'm gonna get slapped for that.*

Her eyes nearly popped out of her head. "Do you even think before you speak?"

"Not always. No."

She smiled and bit her lower lip. "I might have a different answer if you knew my name."

Stubborn? No—more like impossible. "We're back to the name thing again, huh?"

"Yes we are."

He sighed and gave in. "So... if I find out your name, you'll go out with me?"

"I'll go out with you— "

"Yes!"

"If—*if*—you remember my name."

"Done." Once he remembered her name, he would never forget it. A horrifying thought rattled his spine. What if her name was Natalie? No. It couldn't be. It just couldn't.

"And you actually use it. No baby, no sweetheart."

"I *promise*." Austin said the word through gritted teeth. He hated making promises. How could he keep a promise if it wasn't accepted?

She looked skeptical, but agreed. "All right, now go away before someone sees you here. I don't want to hear any rumors about us."

Before she could move, he grabbed her shoulders and pulled her close, planting a hot hard kiss right on her lips. "We're gonna have a lot of fun, sweetheart."

He ducked and ran before she could smack him.

***

"What's wrong with your face?" Sara shifted her backpack and scowled at Jane.

Jane giggled like a giddy schoolgirl dreaming about her first crush, picturing Austin jogging into the locker room. "Nothing's wrong." She bit her lip but the smile would not go away.

"You were with *him*." The nasty curl of Sara's lip and the disgust dripping from her voice left no doubt as to which *him* she meant.

"No...." She couldn't lie to her best friend. "Yes. Just a little."

Sara huffed. "There's no such thing as a little Austin Sinclair. It takes every ounce of energy to keep up with him, and all your strength to pull yourself back together when he moves on."

"How do you know that?"

"Every girl on campus knows that." Sara shrugged and her backpack slipped to her elbow. She snarled and flung it over the other shoulder.

Even Jane knew what Austin could do to a girl. She'd already felt the effects.

When he'd whistled at her, she'd wanted to obey his every command. When he'd called her his girl, she'd wanted to melt in his arms and confess that she wanted him. When he'd admitted he'd spoken without thinking, he'd actually blushed and, wow, that had curled her toes. He'd looked like a naughty little boy caught with his hand in the cookie jar.

Jane had smiled and decided not to cuff him upside the head. That's how he got away with it. He was just too cute to stay mad at.

"It's just a little crush. I'll be over him before he's over me." She was lying to her best friend, but at least it erased the disapproving snarl from Sara's face. Jane decided not to tell her about her little arrangement with Austin just yet.

"You should be so lucky." Sara looked at her watch. "I gotta get to class. I'll see you in the library later."

"Bye."

Jane shook her head, trying to shake the smile off her face. Austin Sinclair certainly wasn't her first crush. She didn't even like his type. She liked smart and serious men focused on the future. That boy was arrogant and irresponsible and focused on the moment.

Yet somewhere deep inside her, the lonely, reckless, bad girl part of Jane came back to life, and hoped Austin would remember her name.

Chapter 3

How the hell could he remember her name? Austin dropped his head back on the pillow. What did he know about her? Long brown hair that felt like silk in his hands, deep emerald eyes that melted him, soft full lips that tasted like strawberries, smooth skin that warmed to his touch, small perfect breasts that begged to be caressed.... Okay, that didn't help, but he sure liked thinking about it. Long legs, the kind meant to be wrapped around his lean waist....

Carrie, the bouncy blonde cheerleader, snuggled closer, sliding her hand under the covers. "I'm not tired."

His *overactive brain* had kept him awake, for once, instead of his *dick*. "Good." He smiled and rolled on top of her, kissing her pretty red lips. She moaned when his hand found her breast, his fingers teasing her nipple.

"Mmm... don't stop."

No way. It would take more than a stubborn brunette soccer player to distract him. He nuzzled his way down to her other breast, but as hard as he tried, couldn't help wondering what a certain pair of perky round breasts would feel like in his mouth. "Hey, baby, do you know anyone on the soccer team?"

"Why are you thinking about the soccer team?"

"No reason." *Not the team, just one player in particular.*

"I know a bunch of the guys: John, Dan, Glenn, Chris, Dave, Eric—"

"Not the guys. The girls' team."

"The girls' team?"

Oops. "Never mind." Austin took her nipple in his mouth before he said anything else stupid.

"You could find a team picture on the school's website."

Ah-ha. Problem solved. Austin smiled at the beautiful blonde in his bed, but imagined the beautiful brunette naked under him, instead. He sighed; the cheerleader would have to go before he could pursue the soccer babe. What was her name again? Carrie? She snuggled into his arms, making herself comfortable in his bed, causing him to stiffen, but not in a good way. He didn't share his bed with anyone—not for longer than necessary, anyway.

He jumped up and pulled his jeans on. "Baby, I think we're done here."

"Mmm...." She reached for him and smiled. "Are you sure about that?"

"Yes, I am."

His serious tone got her attention. "What do you mean?"

"I mean we had fun while it lasted, but it's over."

"I see." Carrie stood up and dropped the blankets.

Austin looked at her flawless naked body—he couldn't help it—but when he didn't respond, she slapped him right across the face.

He'd seen that coming, and deserved it, so he didn't flinch. Girls had slapped him before, so nothing new here. "I'm sorry, but—"

"You're not sorry. You already have another girl eagerly waiting, don't you?"

He didn't argue.

Carrie snatched up her clothes, yanking her shirt over her head. "All my friends warned me about you." She pulled up her jeans and gave them a hard zip. "They said you wouldn't stick around. They said you were great in bed but lousy in relationships."

He didn't argue with that either.

The angry girl grabbed her coat. "Someday, Austin, you're going to meet a girl who will keep your interest for longer than—" She looked at her watch. "—longer than this."

"I doubt it."

Carrie shook her head. "I just hope you realize it before you break her heart." And with that, the bouncy blonde cheerleader walked out of his life.

Okay, that went about as he'd expected, but it had to be done. Austin would not—under *any* circumstances—cheat on a girl. Something his mother had said once, a long time ago, stuck with him: *Don't make her cry.* He rarely made girls cry. Mostly he pissed them off, but he could handle that.

He sat down at his desk and turned on his computer. Yeah, he had another girl waiting... sort of. She might not want him yet, but he'd overcome her objections easily enough. But he wouldn't get anywhere with her—eager or not—until learning her name. He looked up the soccer team's website and found her—sexy librarian glasses, pinned-up, messed-up hair, and a smile that hardened his resolve, among other things.

Austin smiled back at her. "Now you're mine, Jane Elliot."

***

"You told him what?"

"I told him I'd go out with him if he could figure out my name," Jane said.

"Oh, that was brilliant." Sara snapped her book shut and peered over the top of her glasses at her friend. "All he has to do is find you in the yearbook."

"I doubt he has one, and I'm sure he has no idea where the library is."

Jane and Sara spent most of their free time in the library, even when they weren't studying, but they rarely saw any of the football players there.

"True," Sara agreed, smirking, "but he can find you on the soccer team's website."

"Oh my God, I hate that picture." Jane held her book up to her face as if that would hide her. "I forgot about that."

"So now you have to sleep with him." Sara cringed.

"*I* never said anything about sleeping with him." She searched her memory to be sure. "*He* did." Her face got warm when she remembered his "castle whore" comment, but even though Jane usually told Sara everything, including her plans for her dream career, she decided to be careful in this instance. "I said he had to take me on a real date."

"Did you tell him you've never had one before?"

"I've had dates," Jane protested. She focused more on school than her social life, but that didn't mean she'd *never* dated.

"Did you tell him you've never had sex before?"

"I have, too."

Sara frowned, took off her glasses, and rubbed her eyes. "Clumsy McWhatshisname does not count."

"Yes he does." No he didn't. The memory of her first and only sexual experience lasted longer than the encounter itself—quick, awkward, and not much fun. "Do you think it matters?"

Jane didn't know why she worried about it. She didn't plan on having sex with Austin, but then, she'd never planned on going out with him either.

"No," Sara said. "He just wants to get laid."

"He can do that anytime. He doesn't need to go to the trouble of taking me out on a date to get lucky." *Wait, that doesn't sound quite right.*

Sara frowned and flipped through another book. "Guys like him like variety. You're something new, and right now, you're a challenge. As soon as a pretty new face comes along, he'll forget all about you."

"Yeah, I know." She really couldn't expect anything more from Austin. "Still, it could be fun while it lasts."

Why not just enjoy it for a change? Maybe her second time would be better. He did tell her they were going to have a lot of fun together.

Sara sighed. "He won't fall in love with you. He's a heartbreaker."

"I don't expect him to fall in love with me. I know better than that. I just want to have a little fun with him. You're the one who told me I need to have more fun."

"Oh, it'll be fun... till he breaks your heart." Sara scowled at Jane. "And then what will you do?"

"Enjoy it while it lasts and appreciate it for what it is." She squared her shoulders and picked up her book, hiding the uncertain smile on her face. Having more fun... good idea. Having fun with Austin Sinclair...?

***

Now that he knew her name, how the hell was he going to find her? Austin looked in all the places he usually met girls, but he'd never seen her in a bar or a classroom before, so why would she be there now? He had to be missing something. *Think, Austin.* Where would a Bayfield Dean's List academic scholarship soccer player hang out?

The library, dumbass. Just like Natalie had in high school. *Great. Where's the library again?* He couldn't remember the last time he'd gone there, having avoided all libraries after his breakup with Nat.

A couple of wrong turns sent him in circles, but he finally found the building. It looked a lot bigger than he remembered—three floors and stacks and stacks of books. *She'd better be worth it. Just fun – no promises.* He smiled, determined to make it worth his time and effort—no matter what.

It took him nearly half an hour, but he finally found her in the basement, searching the stacks for a book that somehow eluded her. Her fingers crawled across worn spines as if touching the books might reveal the one she wanted. She didn't look up, so he leaned against the bookshelf and watched her. Her glasses were perched on top of her head, and a few strands of her hair tumbled loose from the knot she kept the rest of it in.

Why didn't I ever notice her pretty face? I need to hang out in the library more often. Bookworms need love too.

Damn it, no. Fun – *not love. Not again.*

When she finally looked at him, he gave her a smile that sparkled in her gorgeous eyes. She waited, but he didn't say a word.

"I will hear you say my name," she said.

He just walked over to her and tucked a strand of hair behind her ear, staring into her eyes so intently she looked away. He put his arms around her and pulled her close. His lips found hers, soft and sweet. She held his shoulders and leaned back against the bookshelf.

"Jane." Kiss. "Marie." Kiss. "Elliot." Kiss.

"Mmm, you are thorough."

"I'm just getting started."

He pressed her into the bookshelf, and slipped his tongue between her lips as his hands explored her body. Her hands did a little exploring of their own, sliding down his back, stroking his muscles through his shirt—light, hesitant touches, as if she wanted more but didn't dare.

Austin couldn't remember all the first kisses he'd given, but this had to be better than any of them. His senses went into overdrive, capturing every touch, every sensation—her warmth and softness, the sweet taste of her mouth, the smell of wildflowers and a little bit of soap on her skin. Her little gasps for breath sounded so sexy, and he couldn't stop peeking at the pretty fringe her eyelashes made on her cheeks.

He should probably stop before getting carried away. Anyone could be lurking nearby, and she'd already warned him not to start any rumors. But he didn't want to stop. Not now. Not ever. *Holy hell, this is not good.*

She put her hands on his chest and pushed back, slowly breaking their kiss.

Keep it casual. He grinned. "Well, that was easy."

"Ugh," she grunted. "It's over before it started." Her eyes narrowed and she pushed him away.

Austin stumbled back against the opposite bookshelf. "Janie, wait! I didn't mean *you* were easy."

She ignored him and stomped off.

"It was easy to find out your name." He ran after her. "That's what I meant." *Holy shit, it's hard to keep up with this girl.*

"Yeah, whatever."

"You're not easy at all." *What will it take to make her happy? Why do I care?*

"So you thought one good kiss would get you out of our date?"

"Good? Damn, girl, that was great." Even by his standards. "I'm not trying to get out of our date. Kissing you was just—I don't know—it seemed like a good idea at the time."

She stopped and turned so fast he nearly fell on top of her. "Got any other good ideas?"

"Yeah, I've got lots of good ideas... and lots of bad ones too." His grin froze when her scary green eyes burned holes through his skull. "Let me take you out tomorrow night, somewhere fun 'cause, believe me, if there's anyone who needs a little fun, it's you, Janie."

"Tomorrow night?"

"Yeah. Tomorrow's Friday, so we can sleep in Saturday morning." He winced as the words came out of his mouth.

Her green eyes narrowed for a second, but then they softened a bit and she smiled. "You can't control your impulses, can you?"

"I don't want to." Austin grinned and braced himself, waiting for her to smack him, but she kissed him on the cheek instead.

"Tomorrow night."

"I'll pick you up at seven and take you... somewhere." All his energy had burned out getting her to agree to a date. Now he had to decide what to do with her... besides the obvious.

"Sounds promising." A hint of worry colored her voice.

"Ah, Janie, I promise you will not be disappointed." *Damn it! What am I doing?*

"You promise?"

"Absolutely." He fought his impulses again, and lost, pinning her against the bookshelf, claiming her lips with a kiss that left them both breathless.

He disappeared among the stacks... and took another half hour to find his way out of the damn library.

***

Jane stood in front of her full-length mirror, analyzing what had to be the fifteenth outfit she'd tried on.

Sara pulled another dress from the closet. "This?"

Jane shook her head. "No, it's too cold for that."

Her friend put the dress back. "I think you've exhausted your options."

They'd spent the last couple of hours trying on everything in her closet and dresser. A heavy sigh came from the closet. Jane bit her lip, determined not to let her roommate's lack of enthusiasm bring her down. She'd hoped her own excitement would rub off on Sara, but no such luck.

Sara frowned at the mountain of clothes on her roommate's bed. "Do you want to go through my closet?"

Jane glanced at the clock. "I don't have time."

She looked back at the mirror, tilting her head as if she would like her reflection better from another angle, in her hot-pink lace bra and matching panties—bold and daring. Maybe Austin would get to see them, maybe not. A tingle shot through her just thinking about it. She'd tried on something sexy, something pretty, something plain. Now she wore something... well, something besides her underwear, at least, although Austin would probably rather have her show up naked. Heat rushed to her cheeks.

"It would help if you knew where you were going." Sara picked through the clothes piled on the bed.

"It would help if I had some decent boobs." Jane grabbed her chest with both hands and shoved her breasts together, trying to create some cleavage.

"Guys like boobs no matter what size they are." Sara picked up a random shirt and tossed it at her friend.

Jane scowled at the mirror, sticking her tongue out at the girl in the frilly dress. *Nope, not it.* She pulled off the dress and tossed it on the bed. Desperate to find something decent, she yanked open her dresser drawer and pulled on her favorite jeans. *Not bad.* She held up the shirt Sara threw at her—fitted, but not tight; simple, but not plain; bold red, but not flashy. *That could work.* She felt good in it. She felt like... Jane Elliot, and not like a girl trying to impress the campus stud.

Maybe she was, but he didn't need to know that. "I think this is it."

"Good." Sara picked up her backpack and her keys. "I have to go. Have fun and stay out of trouble." She offered a weak smile and left.

Jane ignored her warning. Maybe a little trouble would be good for her.

She'd felt Austin's presence in the library before she'd seen him. Her skin had tingled where his eyes touched her. No other man had ever looked at her like that. And when he'd called her Janie.... *Oh wow.* Jane had shivered. No one had called her Janie since she was six years old. She'd hated it then, but Austin made it sound so sexy. That's how he made her feel, too: sexy.

One more look at the mirror and.... *Shoes!* She searched her closet and found a pair of high-heeled boots she'd bought months ago, but had never had the courage to wear. Giving in to a rare impulse, she slipped them on and stood up—a little shaky, but not too bad. The four-inch heels made her legs look longer, and gave her butt a nice boost. She felt so good in them, sexy and a little bit naughty. She felt like... Janie.

Bad girl Janie nodded her approval.

A quick look at the clock revealed that she had *ten minutes—ack! Hair!* She twisted it into a knot but that looked too severe, so she flipped it over her shoulders and let it fall down her back. Much better. Jane had to wear her glasses; she couldn't see without them. Hmmm... sexy librarian lets her hair down? She hoped so. Another look at the clock: seven minutes. She dashed to the living room and flipped through the channels while she waited for him, shivering as she relived their kiss.

His hands had wandered over her body as if he owned it. She should've stopped him, but instead her fingers had slipped between the buttons on his shirt, and she'd touched his bare chest. If she'd let him continue, he would've had her naked before their first date, and then it would've been over. She wanted this—whatever it was—to last as long as it could.

A brief flicker of doubt taunted her. *Austin is not the guy you take a chance with.* Sara's warning rang in her ears. He would show up, right? Maybe he'd played her, and would leave her waiting while he laughed at his cruel joke. No, he wouldn't kiss her like that and not finish what he'd started. If nothing else, Austin Sinclair never left a girl wanting.

***

Austin turned on the water and swore when the cold blast hit him in the face. He needed it, though. Having spent the whole day thinking about where to take Janie—and what to do with her—a cold shower would do him some good. The water slowly turned warm as he stood under it, letting it run though his hair, dripping down his back, and flowing over his chest. He closed his eyes and imagined that, instead of water, Janie's fingers were sliding over his naked skin, caressing his shoulders and his arms, stroking his thighs.

Why couldn't he stop thinking about his Janie? His Janie. Austin smiled. He could picture the look she would give him for that—disapproving eyes but a tiny smile. That was one of the things he liked about her. She didn't let him get away with his usual tricks. He wouldn't know her name if she hadn't forced him to find out. He could've seduced her in the locker room or the library if she hadn't made him take her out on a real date.

He liked that too.

He enjoyed spoiling women and did it with pleasure. Some girls jumped into his bed without much pursuit or persuasion. Not that he complained, but he appreciated a good chase every now and then. The only question was how long he should let the pursuit go on. Should he capture her tonight or let her tease him a bit longer? He wanted to enjoy this girl as long as he could, and right now he was having too much fun to let it climax—Austin grinned—so soon.

A drop of water trickled into his ear, and he shook his head. *Call it off now before you get hurt again.*

What? He poked his head out of the shower. The empty bathroom remained silent, and the locked door gave no clues. Where had that voice come from? He pounded the side of his head with his palm, making sure no more bubbles lingered.

"She's not Natalie," he reminded himself, and anyone else who might be listening. By the time he got out of the shower and got dressed, Jack had breakfast burned beyond recognition, along with the kitchen stove.

Jack took one look at dressed-up Austin and groaned. "Is your date tonight with the same girl you met the other day?"

Austin gave him a blank look.

"The girl whose name you couldn't remember?"

"That narrows it down."

"Good point." Jack laughed. "The one from the girls' soccer team."

"Yeah. You owe me a six-pack."

"It's in the fridge."

Austin laughed and picked up a football, tossing it between his hands. It would have been an easy move any other day, but now it bounced off his fingers and hit Jack's arm. "Damn it. Sorry."

"Nervous?"

"Why the hell would I be nervous?" The football somehow bounced away from Austin and rolled across the floor. He grabbed it and slapped it on the table. "Stay."

"She's not Natalie."

"Huh?" The ball rolled off the table and smacked Austin's foot. "Were you listening...?"

"To what?"

"Never mind." Austin shook his head and fished the ball out from under the table.

"And you're not the same guy anymore. You have goals and direction now."

"Yeah, but is it good enough?"

Jack looked straight at him. "For her or for you?"

"What the hell does that mean?"

"Natalie dumped you because she thought you had no ambition."

"Thank you so much for reminding me."

"She thought you'd get injured playing football and have nothing to fall back on."

"She was right. I got hurt." Austin rubbed his knee.

"She was wrong. You have a new dream now."

"Yeah, funny how that works."

"The only question is: is it enough to get you over those bad memories?" Jack grinned. "Or do you need help from someone else?"

"What the hell are you talking about?"

Jack laughed. "I've watched you get ready for more dates than I can remember. I get the feeling this girl is different."

"She's not my usual type."

"True, but I think it's more than that."

"I think you think too much."

Jack's words rushed at him like a runaway train, and the emergency brake dangled just out of Austin's reach. Janie's natural, easy beauty put her in a class above the girls he knew. The more he thought about her, the more he realized Jack could be on the right track. She was different. She resisted him, and he liked that. Her deceptively pretty face had caught his attention, but her strength and determination held it. *She* kept *him* coming back for more.

Natalie had made him feel like that... until she'd called him a dumb jock and said he wasn't good enough for her.

Whoa, Austin, stop right there. His brain screeched to a halt, and he turned to Jack, his jaw set. "I had to work to get her to go out with me. That's all there is to it."

Jack nodded. "That's a start."

Austin rolled his eyes and then smiled. "Don't wait up."

He hadn't decided if he'd bring Janie home or not, but he'd be ready for any possibility.

Chapter 4

When Janie opened her front door, Austin barely recognized her; but when she smiled at him, his heart flipped and he knew he'd found the right girl. Wearing jeans that fit her like a glove, and a rich red shirt that highlighted her luscious brown hair, she'd stand out in any crowd. She met him in the hallway, her eyes almost level with his. *This is new.* His gaze traveled down her long slim legs. Oh, how he loved a woman in heels.

Janie stood up tall in those four-inch heels and met his eyes straight on. "I'm ready."

"Are you sure about that, Janie?" He wanted to rip her clothes off right then, but no, he would wait... for now.

"Yes I am."

They walked out to the crowded parking lot. Did she realize she turned all the guys' heads? Didn't matter because she was with him tonight. No one else could have her.

"That's good to know." He wanted to kiss her again but not here—too many people around to do it the way he wanted to. He may not have cared about what other people thought of him, but he remembered that she did.

"Let's go." He took her hand and led her to his old, beat-up Jeep Wrangler. Before he'd left to pick her up, he'd taken the faded vinyl top off, because he wanted to see her with the wind in her hair. He wasn't disappointed.

She tried to grab her flying hair and twist it, but the wind made it impossible, so she just flung it over her shoulders and brushed it away from her face. "So where are we going?"

"You are absolutely beautiful." He had to tell her that before he did anything else.

"Oh." She blushed and looked away. "Thank you."

His eyes swept over her body and he nearly ran a red light.

"Maybe you should pay attention to the road."

"Yeah, good idea." The Jeep screeched through a right turn. "We're going to The Strike Zone. Have you been there?"

"I've always wanted to go, but I haven't done it yet." Jane shrugged.

"Then this will be a lot of fun." That's what he'd promised her. The Strike Zone's batting cages, pitching, food, and beer provided the perfect place for an action-packed first date.

She laughed. "I should've guessed. I just can't imagine you sitting still through dinner and a movie."

"Nope. You're lucky I can wait to get my hands on you."

"Am I?"

He saw a flash of anger in her eyes, but her tone made him wonder if maybe she wanted him as much as he wanted her. "Yep, you're a lucky girl, Janie."

"Why is that?"

He parked the Jeep and turned off the engine, and looked at the woman sitting next to him. Her serious green eyes challenged him from behind those sexy glasses. She wanted something from him, but he had no idea what. He wanted... well, that baffled him too. He wanted to get her into bed, no doubt about that, but he couldn't shake his longing for more. But more what? And why did he want to risk that again? Jack said Janie wouldn't hurt him the way Natalie had, but how could he be sure?

She kept staring at him. Damn if she wasn't as persistent as he was. Austin liked that.

"No, I'm the lucky one." He smiled and kissed her. He felt her sigh and his heart pounded as though he'd just thrown a 50-yard touchdown pass.

They found a table and ordered some wings and beer, and just as Jane was licking the last of the barbeque sauce from her fingers, Austin nodded toward the batting cages. She shrugged and followed him.

The football star picked up a bat and gave it a few swings. "Prepare to be impressed." He winked at her.

She smiled as he sent the very first pitch sailing over the wall. *Home Run*, the scoreboard jingled and danced.

"Lucky shot."

"Ha." Austin grinned and handed over the bat. "Your turn."

Jane let the first pitch go by. She swung hard at the second one, sending it into the backdrop with an impressive thud. *Standing Double,* the scoreboard flashed.

"Nice," Austin let out a low whistle. "Let's see that again."

"No problem." She hit the next pitch foul, but the one after that was another double. The pitching machine spit out a streaking fastball. She swung hard and sent it sailing into the backdrop—*Home Run.*

"Oh, Janie, you sure know how to get a guy excited."

She laughed and tossed the bat to him.

Austin couldn't be outdone by a girl. He waited for the pitch, swung hard, and missed.

Jane nearly fell over laughing. "What's the matter? Can't handle a bat when you're excited?" Her eyes sparkled.

"Woman, you are asking for trouble."

"Oh, I found trouble the moment I met you."

"That's true. Are you flirting with me?"

She winced. "If you have to ask, I must not be doing it right."

He put his hand on the small of her back, guiding her to the pitching cage. "Let's see what kind of an arm you've got."

A mysterious smile twisted her lips, and as soon as she picked up the ball and got into her stance, Austin knew he was in trouble. She sent a fastball toward the middle of the strike zone and, at the last second, it curved down and away, just catching the corner. *Strike one.*

"I remember you." A touch of awe colored his voice. "You're the girl who struck out half the guys' baseball team in practice last spring."

"Yes." Jane blushed. "You were one of those guys, weren't you?"

"Yes I was."

His embarrassment disappeared. Admiration for her athletic skill made him proud to be with her. Natalie had never respected sports. She'd always thought he was just playing games. Janie understood why he played because she did too. He smiled and watched her throw strike after strike. Even in those heels, her form looked flawless, her motion pure poetry.

"You're the star pitcher, and I'm the star quarterback." He wanted to drop to his knees and worship her amazing stance as she rocked back, preparing to throw another strike. "Hell, we're perfect for each other."

Just a bit outside.

Jane blinked and looked at him, her eyes wide.

"What more could a guy ask for?"

"How about a little humility?"

"Nah." He shrugged. "Humility is overrated. When you're good, you're good."

Gorgeous green eyes blinked at him over the top of her glasses.

"And when you're bad...." His gaze swept her body. "You're even better."

He took the ball from her hand and tossed it aside, sliding his hands into her hair as he pulled her close and kissed her. She resisted just a little bit, as a few people glanced in their direction, but still, her body melted into his.

Why couldn't he stop kissing this girl? He knew he should. People started to stare, but he couldn't get enough. Her warm lips lingered on his mouth as if they belonged there, and her soft body fit like it was made for him.

When someone yelled, "Get some, Austin," he pulled back and growled. *If I find out who did that....* He looked at Jane and winced. "I'm sorry."

"I'm not." She smiled at him and stroked his right arm, keeping him close to her. "Show me what you've got, quarterback."

"Oh Janie." *Football. She means football, idiot.* "I'll show you anything you want."

"I want to see how good you really are." She smiled at him, and Austin caught a hint of mischief in her eyes.

Damn it, this is torture! "You *are* talking about football, right?" He usually did the teasing, but he enjoyed being on the receiving end for a change.

"For now."

They stopped in front of the football cages. That sneaky little devil knew exactly what she was doing, even if he didn't. "As you wish."

He picked up a football and slammed it between his hands, reveling in his element. His first throw was short, quick and dead-on accurate. Twelve yards. First Down.

"Not bad," Jane said.

"Just wait till I get warmed up." The next pass had more power behind it. Fourteen yards. A crowd gathered to watch him.

"You have an audience."

Mostly female, he noticed, but that didn't matter. He just wanted Janie to watch. "I'm used to it."

Each pass got longer and stronger. Twenty-one, twenty-seven, thirty-two yards. He launched a rocket into the center of his target. Fifty-two yard touchdown pass! The crowd cheered.

"You *are* good." She smiled and watched as his friends and fans congratulated him. They loved their quarterback for good reason.

"Thank you, Janie. That means a lot to me." She was proud of him. Proud of him! That felt better than all the praise heaped on him by people he barely knew. Maybe he *was* good enough.

He shook a few hands and accepted some pats on the back, then shooed the crowd away and reached for her. "Come here and let me show you how it's done."

He pulled her into his arms and turned her back against him, so he could show her how to hold the ball. Guiding her arm, he whispered instructions in her ear, pressing his lips closer than he needed to.

She followed his orders and threw for fifteen yards on her first try.

"Great job." He swatted her behind and braced himself for a reprimand.

"You're a great teacher." She smiled and kissed him.

"You're a natural." He couldn't believe he'd gotten away with that ass slap.

"When you're good, you're good."

He laughed. "This is a new experience for me."

"What's that?"

"I've never dated an athlete before. I've only gone out with girls who throw like girls."

Jane smiled and threw a short fast pass directly to the center of the target. "You mean cheerleaders aren't real athletes?"

"Not the ones I go out with. They're more like... entertainment."

She winced.

"Bad choice of words, I know."

"Yeah, but at least you're honest."

"That's true." He put his hands on her hips and showed her how to put more torque into her throw. "I don't lie and I don't cheat." His body matched her motion, his groin rubbing against her ass. *Damn, that felt nice.* "I always break up with a girl before I go out with someone else."

"Oh that's comforting." She rolled her eyes and picked up another football. "So you've never been with two girls at once?"

"Well, there was this one time—" He shut his mouth so fast he nearly bit his tongue off. "Shit. Did I say that out loud?"

Jane turned and looked at him over the top of her glasses, and laughed. "Honest to a fault."

"My only fault." For some reason, talking to her came a little too easily. He knew she meant to give him an intimidating stare, but it was damn sexy too.

"Don't expect me to tell you what mine are."

"I can't find any, and believe me...." He offered his most wicked grin. "...I've looked close."

When she turned and reprimanded him again with her eyes, his arms tightened around her waist and he drew her in close. "The only problem I have with you is that you get all stiff when I kiss you in public." His lips touched hers, and her body went rigid just as he knew it would. He would have to fix that.

He pulled back and ran his hands up and down her back, trying to ease her tension. "Relax," he whispered.

Her lips parted but she didn't say anything. He took that as an invitation and kissed her again, still stroking her back. Her body went limp and he pulled her closer.

"That's my Janie," he whispered against her lips. He looked into those soft green eyes, but as he moved to kiss her again, something made him pause. "What is it?"

"Hmm?" She wouldn't look at him.

"You want to say something."

She bit her lower lip. "Um...."

"Talk to me. Don't be afraid."

Her body got tense again, and when she finally spoke, he barely heard her voice. "Let's go someplace more private."

He nodded. "Okay." He knew what that meant when other girls said it, but Janie was mystifying.

"I don't like having an audience."

He smiled and gave her one more hot kiss—just for the hell of it—and then they left.

***

Talk to me, he said. *Don't be afraid,* he said.

But Jane was afraid. Afraid of what might happen if she admitted to him, or even to herself, what she wanted. She wanted him—all of him—but would never have him. Not really. So she would take what she could get. Even without knowing exactly what would happen, she wanted to take the chance.

They drove to a quiet park near the campus, with no other cars and only a few people—couples making out in the dark. Austin turned off the engine and looked at her, his eyes glittering in the dark. The silence raised goose bumps on her skin, and she stiffened in her seat, twirling her hair around her fingers.

Now you have to sleep with him. Her heart pounded out Sara's prediction. *Have to? No. Want to? Big possibility.*

She looked around, trying to figure out if his Jeep had enough room to have sex in, but with his long arms and long legs, it looked pretty much impossible.

"You're so cute when you're nervous." He leaned close, touching her rigid arm.

"So are you." *Oh good one, idiot.*

He laughed. "Mmm... a smart ass. I like that in a girl."

His smile was just short of heaven, but his blue eyes promised all sorts of sin. What had she gotten herself into?

She shoved the door open and jumped out of that suffocating Jeep. "Let's go for a walk."

A cool breeze blew through her hair, and she took a deep breath. The moon rose over the horizon, casting a silver shimmer on their perfect night. She couldn't think of a thing to worry about.

What about tomorrow, an annoying voice whispered in her head. *Tomorrow doesn't matter. Enjoy now.*

Austin offered his hand and she took it, following him down a rocky path by the river. She walked beside him, leaning against his arm when the path got narrow. She wobbled a bit and he caught her.

"Stupid heels."

"Come here." He found a big rock and sat down with her between his legs, her back leaning against his chest. He wrapped his arms around her waist and rested his chin on her shoulder. "Comfy?"

"Yup." He buried his nose in her hair and breathed deep.

She felt him relax. She couldn't remember him ever being so quiet, but she didn't worry. *Wait... is he humming? Could Austin Sinclair be content? Is such a thing even possible?*

"Why do you hate your name?"

Austin stiffened. So much for being content. Maybe she should've started with a less probing question.

"It's my father's name." The night breeze carried his tense words away, and she leaned close to listen.

"Oh." That couldn't be good.

"My father is... not a nice guy."

No, not good at all. "I understand."

"He cheated on my mother. I don't know how many times. He finally left her for a pretty face half my mother's age." His voice got louder and picked up strength. "Cheated on *her* too. I think he's on wife number four now."

"I see." He'd told her much more than she'd bargained for, but if he wanted to talk, she would listen.

"I know you're thinking that I'm just like him." He let out a sigh. "I guess I am."

His admission surprised her, and she couldn't believe he kept talking.

"But I won't ever make the mistake of committing to one woman. I couldn't live with myself if I broke her heart... if someone got hurt." He said the words with conviction and a hint of something. Grief, perhaps?

Should she point out the obvious? "And yet you're known as the campus heartbreaker."

He chuckled. "How's that for irony? I never make promises I can't keep. I won't fall in love, and no one gets hurt."

He won't fall in love. That's exactly what Sara had said. How did she know him so well? "Love doesn't have to hurt."

His eyes questioned her.

"Love can heal."

"Ha." He snorted.

"Look at my family. My mother is a super-religious, overprotective, uptight control freak. She's afraid I'm going to meet a guy and not finish college like she did, so she doesn't approve of anything I do, and she's constantly judging me."

"You're telling me that doesn't hurt?"

"It hurts a lot. But instead of trying to protect me from the 'sinful world,' my dad sent me out into it. My mom wanted me to stay home and study all the time—and I mean *all the time*—but my dad got me involved in sports. He taught me to play baseball, took me to games, and even let me have a sip of his beer."

"Way to go, Dad."

"My mother did not approve. It was a constant battle between them."

"So your parents hated each other."

She shook her head. "Not at all. They loved each other like crazy."

Austin frowned. "How is that possible?"

"I don't know." Jane had to think about that. "It just worked out for them because they were right for each other."

He laughed. "That only happens in the movies."

"They balanced each other. She worried about everything, and he worried about nothing. She felt guilty all the time, while he laughed and enjoyed life. They were good for each other."

Silence descended, and she jumped when Austin finally spoke. "You're talking about the past. Something bad must've happened to them."

Her voice caught in her throat. "My dad was killed in a car accident two years ago." Tears suddenly flowed down her cheeks.

"Oh, Janie, I'm so sorry." He gently rocked her.

"After he died, my mom thought she was being punished for all the fun she had with him, so I told her something he once said to me."

"What's that? Love is all you need?" He sneered.

She ignored that. "He said falling in love with her was the best thing that ever happened to him, and he wished she believed that too."

"Did she?"

"Yes, but it was too late." She scowled and plucked the grass beside her, yanking it from its roots and tossing it aside. "She's still judgmental and overprotective."

"And that's why I don't believe it. If love healed her, then why does she still hurt you?"

Jane bit her lip, pitying the girl who ever fell in love with Austin. That would hurt more than anything. Another tear escaped her eyes.

He brushed her cheek with his thumb and whispered softly, "Hey, why are you crying on our first date? I haven't even looked at another girl."

That earned a little smile from Jane. "It hurts to know you think love is so worthless. Don't you ever get lonely?"

Pain and loss flickered in his eyes, but he glanced away. When he looked back at her, his usual naughty grin had reappeared. "There are plenty of cheerleaders around to keep me company."

"I don't believe that."

"Not enough cheerleaders? Maybe I'll start dating the women's soccer team."

Jane punched his arm and he laughed. "I can change your mind."

"Think so, huh?"

"I'll prove to you love doesn't have to hurt."

"Good luck with that."

"You don't think I can?"

"No one can." But even as he spoke, he pulled her closer. "I decided a long time ago that love is not an option."

She sighed. "I guess I should be careful what kind of questions I ask you. I forgot how honest you are."

That comforted her somewhat. Sara had said a lot of bad things about Austin, but she'd never once said he lied.

"Don't ask questions you don't want answered." His voice warned her, but his eyes played.

But he was hiding something else... something he didn't want her to see.

"Maybe we should keep walking." She stood up and wobbled, nearly tumbling down the riverbank.

Austin grabbed her arms and held her steady. "Are you sure you can handle this trail in those shoes?"

"I can take them off."

"Or I can carry you."

She squealed as he picked her up and tossed her over his shoulder. "Austin, put me down!" She laughed and pummeled his back with her fists.

"Nope." He spanked her wiggling ass. "Hold still, will ya?"

Jane slapped his butt, giggling when he flinched.

"Woman, you are in trouble now."

She pushed up on his shoulders, but the shift of her weight made him stumble and fall forward into the grass. Austin tried to catch himself, but he fell, still holding her tight.

She grunted when he landed on top of her. "Ow."

"Are you okay?" He raised himself up on his hands, looking down at her.

Chapter 5

"Yeah." She gasped for breath. "Are you?"

"Yeah, you broke my fall." Austin grinned, pressing hard against her.

Jane felt something between them—not like that—she actually felt his—yeah, that—and the evil grin on his face told her he felt it too. Did she dare tell him? She knew he would like it, but then he would know she'd noticed, and she didn't want to go there yet. Good thing her mouth decided not to cooperate. She fought off the temptation to find out what would happen if she said something provocative.

"Glad I could help." She squirmed beneath him, trying to move into a position less... intimate.

Austin smiled and moaned when she wiggled her hips.

"Are you enjoying this?"

"Oh yeah."

He smiled down at her, and for a split second, she wanted to slap that naughty grin right off his face. Then those wicked blue eyes met hers, and her anger turned into another kind of passion. Her hand landed on the back of his neck and she pulled him down for a kiss.

His arms tightened around her body, lifting her up into him as he pressed down, pinning her against the ground. He rocked against her—slowly, gently—and she wondered if he knew he was doing it.

Should she make him stop? No, she didn't want that. Should she move with him? Mmm... that seemed like a good idea. He felt so good—hard, warm, strong. Yes, she definitely wanted more—more kissing, more touching, more of his body against hers.

She moaned into his mouth, arching against him as his body tensed and his maddening motion stopped. "Who's the stiff one now?" She was asking for trouble, but she didn't care.

Austin looked into her eyes, and she stared right back. He shifted his weight, leaving no doubt about how much he wanted her. "Is this what you want, Janie?" He ground his hard cock between her thighs. "I can give you exactly what you're asking for, and I can give it to you all night long."

She bit her lower lip and he sighed.

"That's what I was afraid of." He kissed her and rolled onto his side, taking her with him. Sliding his hand into her hair, he gently pulled her head back, exposing her throat to his mouth.

Jane sighed and cuddled closer to him. She played with the buttons on his shirt, wondering if she should open one. Heat seared her through his clothes, but she wanted to feel his skin. His tongue made circles on her neck just below her ear, moving slowly down her body to the top button of her blouse. She held her breath, hoping he would rip it off with his teeth, but instead, he kissed his way back up her neck, driving her crazy. When he kissed her lips again and ignored her silent wishes, she decided to open the damn button herself.

Before she could do it, he took her hand and moved it to her ribs, entwining his fingers with hers--a sweet, romantic gesture, but she wasn't in the mood for sweet and romantic. She pushed him onto his back and straddled him, leaning over to kiss him hard. She smiled when he moaned.

"Ah, Janie." He sat up, keeping her in his lap with his arms wrapped around her, and touched his lips to hers. She fiddled with his buttons and he grabbed her hands, kissing her fingertips one by one.

She caught her breath. Even a simple sweet kiss from him melted her to her toes.

"Janie, sweetheart, baby, I think it's time to call it a night."

"What?" Bayfield's bad boy wanted to go home early? Alone? Maybe he didn't sleep with every girl he met, after all. "Why?"

"It's getting late."

Right then Jane realized she wanted to sleep with him. She knew she wouldn't see him again after tonight, but hoped tonight would at least last till morning. "Tomorrow is Saturday." She kissed him. "You said we could sleep in."

He chuckled. "I did say that, didn't I?"

He didn't seem to want her. She suddenly felt hot, and the stars started to spin. He'd played her all along.

"I see." She stood up on wobbly legs. He held her arms to steady her, but she jerked away from him. "Take plain Jane out on a date, get her all hot and bothered, and then dump her. Haha. Good joke." She ran away from him, not caring that the Jeep was waiting in the other direction.

"Janie, no!" Austin ran after her. "It's not like that at all."

"Really?" She turned around but kept walking backwards. "Austin Sinclair actually knows how to say no?" She ran off again.

"Janie, wait."

"Don't call me that. Ever."

"Get back here, woman. Let me explain."

She stopped in her tracks, and turned to face him with arms crossed. "This better be good."

He caught up to her and reached his arm out, but she backed away, prompting him to raise his hands in surrender. "I want to take you out again."

She huffed.

"Did you have fun tonight?"

"Till now."

"So did I. We had a great time. Admit it."

She set her jaw and shook her head.

"Damn stubborn woman." He swore under his breath. "I had a great time watching you pitch and teaching you how to throw a football. I even had a great time talking to you. I've never done that with anyone before."

Jane pressed her lips together, trying to stop the smile from taking over.

"I could take you to bed with me tonight, and believe me, I want to." Austin moved closer to her and put his hands on her shoulders. "And you know that."

His soft, husky tone made her shiver as he pulled her against him. She didn't resist.

"I think if we slept together tonight, it could ruin whatever it is we have here."

"You want to wait? Why?"

"I don't know what's going on." He shook his head as if he couldn't believe it either. "But I want it to last as long as it can."

Could she trust him? He flirted entirely too much and said outrageous things, but as far as she knew, he'd never lied to her. "I do too."

"Good, then let me take you out again sometime next week. No, you tell me—when, where. It's all up to you."

She finally smiled. "You're taking a big chance, you know."

"I'm not afraid of you."

"You should be." She loved teasing him.

"I'm not afraid of you... Janie." He ducked and ran.

She tried to run after him, but she stumbled in those shoes.

"Do I have to carry you back to the Jeep?"

"Just don't drop me again."

"Don't tempt me." Those sinful blue eyes sparkled. "I liked where I landed."

"I'll bet you did."

He scooped her up in his arms. "You did too, Janie. You were all over me. You're a bad girl."

She opened her mouth to argue, but couldn't. "I'll deny it. You can't prove anything."

"Don't worry." He kissed her with soft, warm lips. "I'll never tell."

"You don't kiss and tell?"

"Nope. All the rumors you heard about me came from someone else."

"You don't brag to your friends just a little?"

He winced. "Maybe just a little, and only to the ones I trust, but I never name names."

She laughed. "Because you can't remember names."

***

They drove back to her apartment, laughing and teasing and kissing at every red light. Austin hummed while he walked her to the door. He didn't want to say goodnight already, and was pretty sure she didn't either. She'd felt so perfect under him—like she belonged there. It would be so easy to take her to her bedroom and rip her clothes off.

This was supposed to be casual and fun. *What the hell am I waiting for?*

He couldn't remember. It would be so easy to let her have her way with him. Too easy.

What's wrong with easy?

He didn't want her to be easy, or like every other girl. He wanted her, no question, but he suddenly remembered his mother's words: *Anything worth having is worth waiting for.*

Janie was worth the wait.

Yeah, think about your mother, Austin. That'll make you wait.

"You kept your promise." Jane pulled him into the darkened doorway.

Her voice snapped him out of his thoughts. "What promise?"

"You didn't disappoint me."

That simple statement answered his questions. He'd told her he'd wait, so he would. End of discussion.

He held her close. "That was an easy promise to keep."

He would take it slow. Maybe he wasn't used to being patient, but he didn't mind waiting for her. Somehow, it felt like the right thing to do. But that didn't mean he had to stop kissing her. *Definitely need more kissing.*

A wicked smile found its way to her lips. "I was hoping for a little more fun, but no, someone decided to go all virtuous on me."

Teasing him like that could lead to all sorts of trouble. He hoped that was what she wanted.

"Ha. It won't last long." If he didn't leave now, he would have her naked right up against her front door. "I promise."

She pressed her body against him, her lips touching his. "Tell me you want me."

"I want you, Janie."

"Good. I just wanted to hear you say it."

He groaned and kissed her, pinning her to the door with his hard body. "Tease."

"Oh, I'm the tease? You're the one who brought me home early." She pulled at him so hard he fell against the door and nearly crushed her.

"I have to leave now...." He pushed away from her, panting. "...or I never will." A lousy excuse, but he didn't know how to explain it to her. He barely understood it himself. Girls usually begged him for a second date, not the other way around.

"And that's a bad thing?"

His foot hit the sidewalk, but he turned and leaped the four steps back to her, and crushed her against the door again. "Janie, you have no idea what kind of bad things I want to do with you."

"Tell me." She breathed hot in his ear.

"No." He kissed her hard, plunging his tongue into her mouth, one hand grabbing her hair, the other grabbing her ass. "I'll show you." But he pushed himself away again. "Later."

He ran down the steps and never looked back.

Chapter 6

"You're home early."

Austin caught the football Jack threw at his head. He fired it back and bounced it off his roommate's chest. "That's why you're a running back instead of a receiver."

Jack grunted. "So there's a girl out there who can actually resist your charms."

"Yup. I finally found her." Not that he'd been looking.

"Off your game tonight?" Jack leaned back on the couch and put his feet up on the coffee table.

"No." He didn't offer an explanation. If word got out he'd decided to go to bed alone, his reputation would be shot. He'd worked hard to earn that reputation; he deserved it.

"So what happened?"

"Nothing." That was the truth. Sort of. He didn't want to ruin Jane's reputation either. The less said the better. He shuffled to his room, and took off his clothes as the green digits on his clock flashed 9:55—too early to go to bed. Thanks to Janie and her wandering hands, he had a ton of pent up energy he needed to do something with. *Hmm... booty call?*

Call Janie.

He shook his head. Why couldn't he stop thinking about her? He must have known a hundred girls. Why could he only think of one? He put on a t-shirt and shorts, then tied his shoes while Jack came in and bounced the football off Austin's leg.

"You're going for a run at this time of night?"

"I gotta do somethin'."

"Why not call Brenda?"

Brenda... the blonde... no, redhead... damn it, why can't I remember her?

"You could try to patch things up with Carrie."

"Too much work." Besides, he didn't want Carrie anymore. He could only think of one girl worth the effort. "No, I need to work out."

"You need to get laid."

No shit, Sherlock. "I will."

"The best way to get over a girl is to replace her." Jack picked up the football and juggled it. "Isn't that what you told me?"

Austin grinned. He didn't want to replace Janie yet. "I don't give up that easy."

"This one's a challenge, huh?"

"Damn right." *Stubborn, funny, smart, smart-mouthed, beautiful, sexy....* "I like a challenge."

"Going out with her again?"

"Yeah."

"Why does she have you so interested?"

That question lingered in his brain. He couldn't remember the last time a girl had turned him down, and he never refused a girl who wanted him, so why go out with her again? He wanted her. No, something else kept him coming back.

Austin didn't have an answer, so he told Jack what he expected to hear. "Because I haven't slept with her yet."

"Yeah, that sounds about right."

Good. At least someone doesn't think me virtuous. Austin shuddered.

He batted the football out of Jack's hands and threw it in the closet. "I better not hear about this from anyone else."

If that got back to Janie, she would think he had only one thing on his mind, and while it was true at the moment, he couldn't stand the thought of her being hurt by rumors and misunderstanding.

"Hey, I don't tell your secrets and you don't tell mine."

Austin nodded. He dashed out of the house and took off down the street, running out to the quiet, peaceful football field. He realized his mistake as soon as he got there. The last thing he needed was peace and quiet; he needed a distraction so he couldn't hear Jack's question echoing in his head.

Why am I so interested in Jane?

He still couldn't believe he'd said no to sex. She wanted him, but all he wanted to do was hold her. The last time he felt like this, he.... The last time had started out well, but hadn't ended that way.

Natalie was his past. Janie was his future.

What? Now. Janie is now. Focus on the moment.

The way he talked to her—wow—a new experience for him. He and Natalie had talked but never like that. Janie had asked questions; she wasn't shy. Even though he'd told her never to use his full name, she'd asked why anyway. No one ever asked about his name. Once he told someone not to use it, no one ever did. That stubborn woman had asked anyway, but even better than that—she'd listened. Without thinking, he'd confessed his deepest secret, his deepest pain, to a girl he couldn't stop holding.

He'd stopped short of telling her about Natalie. Janie didn't need to know about his heartbreak and humiliation.

Then she'd told him her secret—shared her pain. A woman in tears typically sent him screaming from the room, but her tears hadn't scared him. The depth of her emotion had touched him, and for a moment, he'd envied the connection she had with her father.

His father, on the other hand....

His mother had warned him, and Austin had done his best not to become his father. But his best wasn't good enough. Love was not an option.

Love doesn't have to hurt. Damn it, now Janie's voice stuck in his head. Since when had it gotten this hard to turn off his brain? He smiled. *Since the moment she first rolled her beautiful green eyes at me.* He closed his eyes and wished—hoped—that Janie had been right.

He took a deep breath and started running around the football field.

***

"Do you want to come to the game with me?" Jane dug through her purse, trying to sound casual, and hoping Sara wouldn't bite her head off.

Her roommate sat cross-legged at the coffee table, scribbling in her notebook. She put down her pen and stretched. "Is it at home?"

"No, it's in Oak Grove, but it's not far. I'm riding with the soccer team."

"Me and a bunch of sports nerds stuck in a car for an hour? No thanks." Sara looked at Jane and winced. "No offense."

"None taken." She zipped her purse and took a hesitant step toward the couch. "I'll miss you."

"When was the last time we went to a game together?"

"It's been a while. We used to have so much fun." Jane grinned and plopped down on the couch. "You loved drooling over the tight ends."

Sara laughed. "No, I like the ball runner guy. What's he called?"

"The running back."

"Right, the running back." Sara stuck the tip of her pen in her mouth and her eyes turned dreamy.

"You can lust over him while I ogle the QB." *Darn it!* She hadn't meant to sound go giddy.

"The quarterback? Oh, Austin." The pen cracked. "I don't think so."

"Yeah, that's what I figured." Jane sighed and walked toward the front door.

"I wish I could be happy for you, honey, but I'm so worried about you."

"You don't need to worry. I can take care of myself."

"I know, but I've...." Sara grabbed a new pen and flipped her book open.

"You've what?"

"Never mind. Have fun."

"I will."

Jane stepped into the hall and closed the door behind her. She hated this awkward tension between them. Was this the price for dating Austin? Her relationship—or whatever—with him probably wouldn't last long enough to cost her a friendship with Sara.

Somehow, that thought wasn't very comforting.

***

"Interception!" Austin leaped off the couch and cheered at the TV.

Jack pumped his fists. "Go, go!"

"Touchdown!" They both threw their arms in the air, laughing and clapping so loud that Austin barely heard his phone ring.

He grabbed it without looking at the caller ID. "Hello? Oh, hey Dad." He rolled his eyes.

Jack fell back in the recliner, laughing under his breath.

"Did you see that interception return?" Charles Austin Sinclair, Jr. quizzed his son.

"Hell, yeah."

"Did you see the quarterback's mistake?"

Austin slapped his hand over his face. *Here it comes.* "He threw it to the wrong guy." He grinned at Jack.

Jack snickered and opened a bottle of water.

"Don't be a smartass, son. He took his eyes off the receiver. I've seen you do the same damn thing. Watch and learn."

"Are you calling for a reason, or are you just trying to piss me off?"

"He's trying to piss you off." Jack stuffed a handful of chips in his mouth and nearly choked laughing when Austin snarled at him.

"I want to come see one of your games."

"I have a game every weekend, Dad. We won yesterday. You could've come to that one."

"Are you playing at home next Saturday?"

"Yes."

"Good. I'll be there."

Sure you will. He shook his head at Jack. "Okay, Dad."

"Did you get lucky this weekend? Got another girl waiting for next weekend?"

He practically heard his father salivating over the phone. "I...." No way in hell was he going to tell his dad he'd turned down an easy lay. "I had a date Friday night, and I'll probably see her again soon."

"The same girl?"

"Yes."

"Wow, she must be a hot piece of ass."

"Don't call her that, Dad." Janie wasn't just a piece of ass. *Damn it, why not?*

"Keep your options open, son, on and off the field."

"Yeah, sure." The idea didn't appeal to him like it used to.

"I expect a great game out of you on Saturday. Scouts could be watching you."

"I always play my best, no matter who's watching."

"Good. See you next week."

Austin ended the call and chucked his phone at the couch.

"The usual conversation, huh?" Jack handed him a beer.

"Said he's coming to the game next weekend."

"Oh joy."

"You know he won't make it."

"I'll take that bet."

Austin sneered and turned his attention to the game, but talking to his dad had sucked all the fun out of it.

"Why didn't you tell him about your early night with Jane?"

"Are you crazy? You know my dad. If I told him I'd called it a night, he'd... wow... he'd freak."

"That would be fun to watch."

Austin laughed. "Yeah. No." He shook his head. "I don't want to find out. I have enough crazy in my head. I don't need him coaching my bedroom sports too."

"Doesn't he already?"

He couldn't argue with that. "Not with Janie. I'm not gonna let him call this play."

"The ball is in your hands. Are you gonna hand it off or keep it and test the defense?"

Austin downed his beer and glared at Jack. "What the hell is that supposed to mean?"

"You know what it means."

"Whatever."

He knew Jack was right. Hand her off to someone else, or hang on and hope he didn't get sacked again?

***

"You told him what?" Sara nearly dropped her oatmeal on the kitchen floor.

"We're going out again." Jane smiled, completely oblivious to the juice overflowing its glass. Funny how her Friday night date made Monday morning so pleasant.

"What the?" Juice dripped from the table onto her pants. "Nice."

Sara shook her head. "Bad idea. Why?"

"Why not?" She mopped up her juice and shot a glare at Sara. She didn't have to explain anything to her. "We had a good time so we decided to do it again."

"Ah, I see." Sara sat down at the table. "You had fun in bed and now you're hooked just like all the other girls he uses."

"We didn't sleep together." She turned on the toaster oven, still puzzled by that.

"Seriously? I thought Austin slept with every girl he went out with."

"I did too, but there's a lot more to him than sex." She couldn't deny that his raw sexuality appealed to her, but Jane kept that thought to herself.

"You're kidding."

"No. He's funny, he's an incredible athlete, and he's a good listener." *And an amazing kisser.* She closed her eyes, remembering the touch of his lips on hers, his hands in her hair, his tongue in her mouth, his body crushing her... hard, hot, burning.... *Smoke? Ack!* The toast was on fire.

"This is Austin Sinclair you're talking about."

"Uh-huh." She turned off the toaster oven and waved the smoke away.

"A good listener?"

"Yeah, that was a total surprise."

"I thought Austin only heard what he wanted to."

"Why are you being so hard on him?" Jane didn't want or need Sara's approval, but a little less judgment would be nice. "You don't know anything about him."

"I know enough."

"Only gossip."

"There's a little bit of truth to every rumor." Sara bit a chunk off the burnt toast and tossed the rest of it across the room into the sink.

"Maybe." Jane suddenly remembered what he was doing (and who he was doing it with) when she'd met him. "Probably."

Yet he'd decided to wait. Why would he do that if he had no interest in her... at least a little bit?

"Maybe he could change." *Darn it!* She hadn't meant to say that out loud. Could she reform the bad boy? Did she want to?

"He'll never change." Sara practically spit the words at her. "Can't you see what he's doing to you?"

She shook her head.

"He's playing you. He wants you to think he's a nice guy because he knows you won't go for the bad boy."

Not entirely true. She hid her smile in her glass of orange juice. Just thinking about his naughty streak made her tingle.

"After he has his fun with you, he'll get bored and go after the next pretty face he sees." Sara stabbed her oatmeal with her spoon, over and over.

Jane almost felt sorry for it.

"Trust me, I know."

Jane's smile faded. "I know what he does. I know he won't stay with one girl." He'd told her he never would. "And I know he'll lose interest in me sooner or later."

"Probably sooner."

"So why can't I just have fun with him while it lasts? Other girls do."

"Lots of other girls."

"Why can't I be one of them?"

"Why would you want to?"

"Because I want to enjoy life for a change. I want to take a risk. I've always been the careful one, doing what everybody else thought I should do. 'Don't do that, Jane, you might get hurt.' 'Do your homework, Jane, you can have fun later.' Well, it's later. It's finally my turn to have fun."

She threw her dishes in the sink. "So if you can't understand that... fine." She grabbed her backpack and slammed the front door behind her.

Chapter 7

Gray clouds gathered in the western sky, and a cold blast of wind ruffled the pages of Jane's textbook, flipping them to the wrong chapter. She sighed and searched for her place again, but the page she read over and over made no sense anyway.

She closed her book and looked at her watch—half an hour until soccer practice. All day long, she'd stewed over her fight with Sara. They'd avoided each other at lunch, as Sara had sat with her friends from the psychology department, and Jane had sat with the soccer team. Bayfield's cafeteria food had churned in her stomach, so she'd gone outside to read, hoping some fresh air would make her feel better.

No such luck.

Her mother's number lit up Jane's cell phone. *Great.* Just what she needed—a side of guilt to go with the cold shoulder she'd had for lunch. She could let it go to voice mail, but she would have to call her mother back eventually. Better to get it over with now.

"Hi, Mom."

"Hello, dear. Were you busy?"

"Not really."

"Were you studying?"

"I was trying to." *Always asking about studying. Does she care about anything else?*

"That's good. How's school?"

"Fine."

"Just fine?"

Her best friend wasn't speaking to her because she hated the guy Jane was dating. Jane had wanted to sleep with him, but he'd said no. Now he wanted a second date, and this time they probably would do it. Did her mom really want to talk about that?

"Yes. Fine."

"All right. How did your midterm exams go?"

"I got an A on the first one." *Tell her that right away to avoid an interrogation.* "And I have another one tomorrow."

"Will you have time to study tonight?"

"Yes, after soccer practice."

"Hm."

She knew that 'hm' all too well. That was her 'I don't approve, and I'm pausing for dramatic effect' hm.

"Maybe you should skip soccer and do some extra studying."

"I know how to manage my time."

"I know you do, dear, but don't forget why you went to that school... so far away from home...."

Escape! "Uh-huh."

"You need to get good grades— "

"I do get good grades, Mother."

"I know you do, but you shouldn't let frivolous things distract you."

Ugh. Her mother sucked all the fun out of her life. "I'm not distracted. I can play soccer, go out on dates, and still pass my exams."

"You're dating?"

Oh crap. "Um... yeah. I'm kinda seeing a guy."

"Seeing?"

"We went out once, last weekend."

Her mother was silent.

"We had fun."

Still quiet.

"He's a fun guy." *Stop babbling, Jane.* She didn't need to know about Austin's kind of fun.

"Fun is not important. You need to focus on school."

"I *am* focused on school."

"Are you going out with him again?"

Absolutely. "I'm thinking about it."

"Then you're not focused on school."

"Yes I am." *This is going downhill fast.*

"Jane, dear, you can't have a boyfriend and keep up your grades."

"Why not?"

"Boys have only one thing on their minds. He won't let you study because all he wants to do is have sex."

Actually, he'd said no when Jane had only one thing on *her* mind. She smothered a laugh when she imagined what her mother would say to that.

"Going out on a date again is a bad idea."

In a flash, Jane re-lived her argument with Sara. Was dating Austin really a bad idea?

"Jane?"

She looked at the phone in her hand as if she'd never seen it before. "Yeah, Mom, I'm here."

"This is exactly what I'm talking about. He already has you distracted. I hope you're not planning on seeing him before your next exam."

"I haven't thought about it." She hadn't thought about anything *else,* especially her exams. *Oh. My. God. Is Mom right? Is Austin too much of a distraction?* She didn't have time for fun, especially not during midterms.

"You need to think about it."

"I will." Jane sighed. She wanted to go out with Austin again, but with graduation only a semester away, she couldn't afford to. She'd gone out with him once and had some fun. Mission accomplished. She couldn't take time away from school to do it again.

"You shouldn't be dating anyone until you finish with school and have a good job."

You shouldn't be dating anyone.... Going out on a date is a bad idea....

The difference between Sara and Jane's mother: Sara didn't want her dating Austin; her mother didn't want her dating at all.

"You need to be able to take care of yourself. Don't make the same mistake I made."

"Mom, I can take care of myself. I'm twenty-two. I'm an adult."

"I realize that."

"I don't think you do. I've been focused on school for the last three years—"

"I'm surprised you could focus at all while going out on all those dates."

"Mom, let me finish. I will graduate this year with excellent grades."

"I hope you can."

"Listen to me, Mom. I can get good grades, play soccer, and go out on dates too." *And have fun doing it!*

"Jane, you can't have everything."

"Why not? I've worked really hard these last three years. I deserve to have a little fun. I've earned it."

"Hard work is its own reward."

"Good lord, Mom, think for yourself for a change."

"You watch your language, young lady."

Jane didn't have time to argue with her so she gave up trying. "Mom, I'm going to practice. I'll study for my exam after that, and I'm going out with Austin again, and we'll have a great time." She packed up her books and headed toward the soccer field.

"Hm. What are you going to do with him?"

Good thing her mother couldn't see the evil smile on her face. "I haven't decided yet, but it doesn't matter. He can make anything fun."

"Oh, Jane, be careful."

Her mother sounded so worried that Jane had to laugh. "Mom, he won't do anything I don't want him to do." *Ugh. Why did I say that?* "Austin's a good guy," she fibbed.

"Hm."

That was her 'I seriously doubt it' hm. "But even if he isn't, I'm going to have fun with him just because I want to."

"That's hardly a good reason to—"

"I don't need a reason." *Good or otherwise.*

"Jane, you need to be responsible—"

"I am responsible!"

Both Jane and her mother stopped and took a deep breath.

"Do you remember what the grief counselor told us?" her mother finally asked.

Jane sighed, "Don't take it out on each other."

"I'm sorry I was so harsh with you, dear. I worry too much. I need to remember that you're an adult, and you make your own choices."

"I'm sorry I yelled at you. I know you worry because you care about me." They were repeating words the counselor had given them, but they worked.

"I love you, Jane."

"I love you, too."

"What's his name again?"

"Huh?" She forgot they'd been arguing about Austin. "Oh. Austin Sinclair. I met him...." *Do not tell her that story!* "...at football practice."

"You play football?"

"No, he does." She laughed.

"Oh, right." Her mother laughed too. "It's nice that you have athletics in common."

"Yeah." Finally, they agreed on something. "I gotta go to practice, Mom."

"All right. Have a good time."

Jane knew her mom had made an effort to say that.

"But remember school comes first."

Back to her old habits. "I'll remember."

"Call me if you need anything, okay, honey? I know how much you miss talking to Dad, and I want to be there for you too."

"Okay." Jane choked as her eyes misted.

She sighed and hung up the phone, glad soccer practice started in a few minutes. After the emotional rollercoaster she'd ridden today, she needed to kick something—hard, fast, and repeatedly.

***

"Gooooaaall!" Austin's voice echoed across the soccer field, stopping Jane in mid-kick.

She smiled as he walked over to her, then she lined up behind a row of soccer balls and kicked each one into the goal without mercy.

"Damn, girl, I hope I'm not the guy who pissed you off."

"Not this time." She lined up again.

"Good." He winced as her foot connected with the ball with a solid thud. "Great legs, Janie." He grinned as his eyes swept over her. "And I mean that in more ways than one."

"Why do guys like legs?" She looked down at hers.

He smiled and stared at her powerful thighs. "Because legs lead to more interesting places."

"Is it always about sex?"

"Yeah, pretty much."

She laughed, then lined up on the last ball and sent it sailing over the goal. "Oops."

"Feel better now?"

"Yeah, a little."

"Rough day?" He followed her to the bleachers.

"I had a fight with Sara this morning. I was pretending the ball was her head." She grabbed a bottle of water and collapsed on the players' bench.

"Ouch. Poor Sara." He sat down beside her. "Who's Sara?"

"My roommate."

"Yeah, roommates can be a real pain in the ass." Austin liked the idea of trading his roommate in for a female model. "What did you fight about?"

A slow smile lit up her eyes. "You."

"Not the first time women have fought over me." He watched as she rolled her eyes. *Jackpot*—exactly the reaction he'd hoped for. "Is she jealous?"

"No. She doesn't like you."

"Yeah, women either love me or hate me."

Jane's smile faded. "And then my mother called."

"Not good?"

"No, it wasn't."

"Did you tell her all about me?"

"I didn't intend to tell her anything about you— "

"But you couldn't help bragging."

"Oh, please!"

Wow, two eye rolls in the same conversation. Bonus points for that. "Yeah, that was a little much, even for me."

"Just a little."

"So what did you tell her?"

"I told her I know how to manage my time."

That didn't sound very interesting. "Uh-huh. And then?"

"And then she almost talked me out of going out with you again."

Holy hell! "Almost?"

"I was this close to getting sucked in by her guilt trip."

"What talked you out of it?"

"She did. If I let her talk long enough, she eventually stops making sense."

Austin laughed. "She sounds just like my dad. We should get those two together."

Jane cringed. "Oh, I think that would be an extraordinarily bad idea."

"Let's just hope your roommate and your mom never get together."

"Sara has never met my mom."

"And yet they both hate me."

"No, Mom just hates the *idea* of you."

"Ah. Big difference." He didn't quite get it, but as long as Janie still wanted to go out with him, he didn't need to.

"It's big enough to keep me from going along on that guilt trip."

"Mmm... I think that means you like me."

She blushed. "Yeah, I like you." She leaned close and brushed her shoulder against his. "Don't worry about them. Sara's just cranky. Mom is... *really* cranky."

"Needs to get laid, huh?"

She gave him a disapproving look. "Sex doesn't solve everything."

"Sex is a part of life. It's not a separate thing. It's normal, natural, fun. It's a lot of fun. It's no different than anything else."

She smiled. "I like that idea."

"Maybe you should give it a try." He bumped his thigh against hers.

"Hey, you chose to go home early."

"I know, I know. Don't remind me."

Jane laughed.

"Have you decided what you want to do for our next date?"

"I have an idea." She bit her lower lip and kicked the grass at her feet.

"Are you gonna tell me about it?"

"Not yet. I need to work out some details."

"Mmm... I like details."

She raised an eyebrow, a hint of a smile tugging at her lips. "You can make anything dirty, can't you."

"It's a gift."

"One of many, I'm sure."

"Would you like to find out?"

"I think you know the answer to that."

Was she undressing him with her eyes, as he'd done to her?

"Come here." He grabbed her hand and led her off to a half-hidden doorway on the far side of the gym. Someone could see them if they looked hard enough, but Austin didn't care about that right now. He suddenly felt the need to kiss her, and he didn't want to wait until she figured out when their next date would be.

He leaned back against the wall, pulled her in close, and held her face in his hands. He touched his lips to hers and slid his hands down her back. She fit against him so tightly that only their damn clothes came between them. If he could do nothing but kiss Janie for the rest of his life, he would die a happy man. He'd have an eternal hard-on, but he would be happy.

Happy without sex? What a weird thought.

Jane squirmed in his arms. He didn't want to let go, but she managed to pull back enough to speak. "Do you know what I like best about you?"

This ought to be interesting. "Let's see... my dashing good looks, my devastating charm, my dirty sense of humor, my—"

She shut him up with a kiss. "Your full-body-contact kisses." She kissed him again, crushing him against the wall. "Please don't ever stop kissing me like this."

"Mmm... my kind of girl." He ran his hands up and down her body. "You're not so stiff anymore."

"You are."

"That's all your fault, you know."

"Really?"

"Oh hell yes!"

Finally, she looked up and smiled. "I like that."

Definitely my kind of girl. "Get used to it."

He wanted to pull her closer, to crawl on top of her and know her from the inside out. He wanted that so much, but he couldn't do it here. Voices approached their not-private-enough location, so he gently pushed her away and nodded in that direction. They pretended to talk about something else until everyone had disappeared.

She moved closer. "I want to... um...." She stopped and took a deep breath. "I want to make dinner for you."

"Wow. I'm impressed."

"Wait till after dinner to say that." She looked away, pink coloring her cheeks. "I just need to find out when Sara won't be home."

"Okay. Just tell me when you want me."

She peered at him over the top of her glasses.

"Yeah, yeah."

"Soon." More people walked toward the gym. "I promise." She kissed him and jogged away.

He ran his hands through his hair and leaned back against the wall. Yep, he would be running around the football field tonight.

Chapter 8

Jane checked the oven timer then scurried back to her bedroom to finish getting dressed. What was she thinking trying to cook for him? She searched through her closet with shaking hands, sprinting back to the kitchen in her underwear when something boiled over. The only other people she ever cooked for were Sara and her parents. They loved her, so they loved her cooking. Austin would be a real test of her ability.

She pulled on her jeans and a fitted shirt with a deep V-neck she'd borrowed from Sara. It showed a little more skin than she usually liked, but she felt like being bold. She decided not to wear her glasses, and when he knocked on the door, she quickly yanked a brush through her hair.

Ack! No time to find shoes. Why did I invite him over so early? A little smile lit her eyes. *Stupid question.*

She ran to the door and looked out the peephole, distracted by an unknown humming noise. A big bunch of flowers covered Austin's face. Jane laughed and opened the door.

Austin's mouth fell open, and for a minute, he gulped like a fish. His bad blue eyes raked over her all the way from her messy hair to her bare toes. "You look good enough to eat." His smile made her shiver.

"Thank you."

"I, um, flowers." He gasped again. "I brought you flowers."

"They're beautiful. Thank you."

"My pleasure." He pulled her close and kissed her, molding his body against hers the way she liked. "No glasses tonight." He kissed her closed eyes.

"I'm near-sighted so I can see things that are close up."

"Then I'll make sure I keep you real close." He bumped his nose against hers.

Jane knew she had something important to do, but when his lips touched her skin, she forgot everything and melted in Austin's arms. *Melt....* That sounded familiar.

A sizzling sound from the kitchen snapped her back to reality. "The butter is burning!" She tore away from him and ran to the kitchen. She rescued the butter, checked the potatoes, flipped the chicken, and put the flowers in a vase.

He caught her as she ran past him, nibbling her neck as she searched the fridge. "Mmm... yummy."

"Stop distracting me or you won't get any dinner."

"You're so tasty." He kissed her until the sizzling started again.

Jane grabbed the hot pan, and her finger bumped the rim. "Ow!" She turned on the faucet and stuck her hand under the cold water.

"Let me take care of that." Austin examined her fingertip. He softly kissed it, pulling it into his mouth and sucking on it. "Better?" His eyes sparkled as his tongue soothed her.

She nodded, breathing hard.

"Glad I could help."

It wasn't what he said so much as the way he said it. His tone dripped with suggestion and his wicked eyes said what his sweet lips didn't.

"You bad boy." She turned back to the stove before he could see her smile.

He put his hands on her hips and turned her around, trapping her against the cabinets. "I think you like me because I'm a bad boy."

She shook her head, biting her lower lip. It didn't seem possible, but he'd found a way to move closer to her.

"I don't think you've had enough bad boys in your life."

"One is more than enough." She braced herself against the counter when he kissed her, letting his hands explore her body.

"Think you can handle me?"

"I'd like to." Oh, the things that came out of her mouth when she talked to this man. She wanted to handle him in all sorts of ways. She wanted to let him be as bad as she knew he could be, and she wanted to be bad with him.

He laughed and lifted her up onto the countertop, standing between her spread legs. He slid one hand under her shirt, stroking her hot skin, while brushing his other hand against her inner thigh, teasing her. "No more waiting. If I wait any longer, I'm gonna explode. That beeping noise is a warning." His hand stopped moving and he looked around.

What the hell? Jane slapped the beeping oven timer, both relieved and disappointed by the interruption. "Dinner's ready."

Austin sighed.

A square oak table and four chairs were tucked in the small space between the kitchen and living room, creating an intimate dining room. Jane set Austin's flowers as the centerpiece, lit a pair of candles, then set two places opposite each other. When she went back to the kitchen, Austin moved his plate to the corner next to hers.

"I won't bite...."

She saw right through those devious blue eyes. "Unless I want you to?"

He laughed when she bit her lip. "Exactly."

"Shut up and pour the wine."

"My pleasure."

She served her favorite, most dependable recipes: chicken with lime butter, mustard green beans, and roasted red potatoes. She couldn't go wrong with that.

"Wow, Janie, this is delicious."

"Thank you."

"Who taught you how to cook?"

"My mother did. Cooking was the one thing she let me have fun doing."

"What else did she not let you do?"

"Where do I start? She wouldn't let me go to R-rated movies. She wouldn't let me listen to rock music. 'It's the devil's music,' she said. She wouldn't let me go to dances. She didn't let me go out on dates till I was eighteen."

"Damn."

"But I did sneak out with my girlfriends a few times. We met up with guys and went dancing and to the movies. She grounded me for two months when she found out."

"Ouch."

"She didn't let me wear makeup, but I borrowed some from my friends' at school, and then I accidentally wore it home one day."

"How long did you get for that?"

"The eye shadow smeared all over my shirt, so I had to do the laundry for a month." That reminded her of another of her mother's rules. "She only let me wear white cotton underwear, so as soon as I went away to college, I bought a bunch of tiny lacey panties and matching bras—"

"Is that right?" His gaze landed on her chest, and his wicked grin stripped her naked.

"Oh. Yeah." Jane crossed her arms over her breasts.

"So why aren't you an uptight prude like her? You seem to be a normal hot-blooded woman. What changed you?"

She took a sip of her wine and thought about that. "I wouldn't say I've changed. I've always been normal and hot-blooded, as you put it.

My mother tried to squelch that, but it didn't take. My dad's family was normal, laid-back and easy-going like him. They had a good time no matter what they did, but my mother constantly judged me. I tried my best to win her approval, but I couldn't do it. After my dad died, I learned to think for myself, and ever since then, I haven't really cared what other people think of what I do."

"And yet you still worry about your reputation here on campus."

She met his eyes and smiled. "Yeah, I still have some issues to work on. I still feel guilty when I have too much fun. I still do things I know my mother wouldn't like, just to spite her. I hope someday I won't care anymore."

Austin downed his wine and refilled their glasses. "Would your mother like me?"

Jane laughed. "Not at all."

"Good."

"Although I suspect you could charm her for a while before she figured out how wicked you really are."

"Yeah, I've been charming women since the day I was born. My mother could never stay mad at me. I just had to smile at her and flash my baby blues, and she would melt."

"Why am I not surprised?"

"I can get away with anything. My sisters hate me for it, but it works on them too."

"Are you the baby of the family?"

"Nope. Middle child, but I'm the only boy."

"Spoiled rotten."

"Yes I am."

"Is your father a charmer like you?"

His smile faded.

"Oh, I'm sorry. I shouldn't have asked about him."

"It's okay." He gulped his wine. "Yes, he is. I learned a lot from him, but most of it comes naturally." He winked at her.

"What else did your father teach you?"

He groaned. "Now that's a question you definitely shouldn't have asked."

"Oh." She bit her lip and looked down at her plate.

His lips formed a hard line as he pushed his chair back and crossed his arms over his chest. "My father taught me that love is for romance novels, Hallmark cards, and getting laid on Valentines' Day. Romance doesn't last, so just have a good time—no strings attached—and no one gets hurt."

She took a bite of chicken and thought about that. "There's nothing wrong with having a good time." Isn't that why she'd decided to go out with him? "But don't you want more than that?"

He gave her a blank look. "Like what?"

"Like commitment, a relationship, someone you can spend the rest of your life with?"

He didn't budge. "Nope."

"Oh, sorry, is that too boring for you?" She scowled at him over the top of her wine glass.

"No, not boring. I just don't think it's possible. I *know* it isn't."

She glared at him, searching his eyes for that mischievous sparkle, but he stared right back at her, completely serious. "I think it's possible."

"Well, that's where you're wrong."

"It is possible if you meet the right person." Her protest was a little more desperate than she'd intended.

He cringed. "And who would that be? I can't possibly be the right guy for you—or anyone. It's not that simple."

"How would you know if any girl is right for you if you don't stick around long enough to find out?"

"My parents—"

"Oh please!" Jane slapped her fork down on the table. "When are you going to stop blaming your parents for your pathetic love life?"

Austin pushed his chair back hard and stood up. "For my what?"

"You heard me." She got to her feet and advanced on him. "Your dad couldn't stay with one woman, so you use that as an excuse to do the same thing."

He stepped back. "It's not an excuse. I like variety."

"Is that what you want?" She stood with her hands on her hips, searching his eyes again for some hint at the truth. "Is variety what makes you happy?"

"Happiness has nothing to do with it." He broke their gaze, turning away from her and running his hands through his hair.

She held her ground. "Really? You're just looking for a good time?"

"A variety of good times." He looked back at her and grinned, but he quickly got serious. "It's who I am, Janie. I am what my parents' pathetic relationship made me." He sighed and put his hands on the back of his chair, leaning on it for support. "If that's not good enough for you—"

Jane shook her head, cutting him off. "I don't buy that. I could've turned into an uptight prude like my mom, but I learned to think for myself. I make my own choices."

"What choices have you made?"

She sat down at the table, took a sip of wine and thought about it. "I chose to play soccer. I chose to go away to school. I chose to be here with you tonight." She looked up at him, her lips pressed together, wondering if she'd made the right choice.

The hard set of his jaw disappeared. "That was your choice? I thought you couldn't resist me."

"Yeah, that might have something to do with it, but remember...." She tried to give him a disapproving look, but couldn't get rid of her smile. "I said no first."

"I remember. I also remember how you couldn't keep your hands off me in the library." His eyes slid down her body. "And in the park."

"You started it." She looked away again.

"You didn't stop it." He sat down and reached across the table, making her look at him. "Tell me you want me, Janie."

"No." She tried to defy him. "You tell me."

"I already have. That's never been a secret." Austin withdrew his hand and met her eyes. "I don't lie. If anything, I'm a little too honest."

"So I've noticed."

"I say what's on my mind, and I don't give a shit what other people think."

"I've noticed that too."

"For example, I think your bare feet are the sexiest part of your body I've seen so far, and I can't wait to see the rest of it." He slid closer, but didn't touch her. "And to get my hands on it. Again."

Her skin got hot and her heart pounded. *Oh God.* One smooth line from him, and she was willing to forget all about their argument and crawl into his lap. "You don't know when to quit."

"Should I?"

She shook her head.

"I didn't think so." He grabbed her behind her knee and pulled her closer, chair and all, and slid his hand up her thigh.

He wanted to sleep with her tonight; she could see it in those gorgeous blue eyes. *Oh God. Oh –* "Damn it."

"What did I do wrong?"

"I forgot to make dessert." Jane hoped he couldn't tell she was stalling. She'd crawled all over him when she knew he wouldn't do anything about it, but now she knew he would, and it scared her.

"You're my dessert." He stood up and held out his hand. "Come sit on the couch with me."

"What about the dishes?" Was he testing her? Did he want to see how far she'd let him go?

"They're not going anywhere. Come on." He took her hand and practically dragged her to the living room.

She sat on the couch the way her mother had taught her to sit in church: straight up, knees pressed together, hands in her lap. Austin sat beside her and slid his hand into her hair, massaging the back of her neck. She tried to let his touch relax her, but it didn't work.

Why am I nervous? Sara wouldn't be home until tomorrow morning, and Jane's bedroom was right down the hall. Jane knew all of that; she'd planned it that way. But for some stupid reason, she could only think about that awkward first time—clumsy groping, sloppy kissing, pain. *It won't be like that with Austin, will it?*

His hand moved in slow circles under her hair, down her neck, across her shoulders. He reached out and touched her face with his fingers, stroking down her cheek until she turned and looked at him.

He didn't say a word, but his eyes told her everything she needed to know. It would never be awkward with him. She relaxed and shifted to a more comfortable position.

He grabbed her ankles and lifted her feet onto his lap, rubbing them one at a time.

"Mmm... you're so good with your hands." She sighed as the tension finally left her body.

"So I've been told." He gritted his teeth. "Red is a good color on you." He stroked her painted toes.

"Thank you."

"Did your mother forbid you to wear nail polish?"

"No, she didn't. That's the weird thing. Her nails were always painted bright gaudy colors. She almost had a fetish for it."

"That *is* weird." An evil smile twisted his lips. "Do you know what I have a fetish for?"

"I'm afraid to ask."

He laughed and ran his fingertips down the center of her foot. "Tickling pretty girls."

"Eek! Don't do that." She jerked her leg away.

He caught her foot again and rubbed it while she closed her eyes and sighed. "Actually, I have a fetish for touching. Girls in general; you in particular." Then he tickled her.

"Stop it." Jane giggled and pulled her foot away again, and tucked it under her.

"You know I can't resist a challenge."

"Try."

"Sounds like a challenge to me." He grabbed her ankle and tickled the bottom of her foot, holding tight as she squealed and squirmed.

"Austin, no!" She gasped and flailed, wrenching her foot free and kicking him in the head.

"Uh," he grunted.

"Oh my God." She scrambled to her knees. "Are you all right? I didn't mean to do that." She gently touched his temple, searching for any permanent damage.

"Yeah." He closed his eyes and leaned back. "Remind me never to tickle a pretty soccer player."

"I'm so sorry. That was a total reflex." Jane scurried to the kitchen, and returned with some ice.

"It's okay." He held the ice to the side of his head. "A kick to the head will probably do me some good."

"I'm sorry."

Austin groaned, but his eyes sparkled just a bit as she frowned and picked up the ice pack. "I don't see any bruising or swelling." She kissed his cold skin.

"I'm kinda dizzy." He slumped sideways, his face landing nicely between her breasts.

His moan sounded a little too happy. He slid his arms around her waist and nuzzled closer, the skin inside the V of her shirt vibrating as he hummed against her. "Feeling better?"

"Mm-hmm." His tongue slipped under her shirt, searching.

His mouth on her skin felt hot and soft, sending little jolts of electricity all through her body. She wanted more. How could she tell him that? *What's holding me back?* Free from her mother's rules, free from her mother's guilt, but her own insecurity still got in her way.

Jane took a deep breath and made up her mind. *Yes.* She wanted Austin, and refused to let anything stop her tonight. She lay back on the couch, stretching out beside him. "You know, if you want to fool around, all you have to do is ask." She draped her legs over his lap, keeping her feet a safe distance from his head.

"Nope." He pressed his lips over her pounding heart. "Why bother asking when I have you right where I want you?"

"Do you, now?"

"Oh, hell yes. Let me show you."

He caressed the length of her body, sliding his hand under her jeans from her bare ankle to her knee. When he couldn't reach any higher, he pulled his hand out and palmed her thigh, slowly rubbing in circles, cupping her bottom and giving it a squeeze before sliding his hand around to her hip. His fingers traveled just under her jeans and stroked her bare stomach. Then he moved his hand up under her shirt instead of down, caressing her ribs, skimming along below her bra.

She held her breath, waiting for him to keep moving up. He did, but over the top of her shirt—not under it as she'd hoped—caressing her shoulders and neck. His gaze followed his fingertips as they traced inside her neckline, down one edge and up the other, exploring her breasts as they rose and fell under his touch. Her body tingled everywhere he touched her. When her eyes met his, he lifted her chin in his wandering hand and kissed her.

His tongue played with hers, and he continued to her neck, tasting her flesh with tiny bites. His mouth moved down, kissing every inch of bare skin he found. Her shirt offered quite a lot of it, but he didn't stop there. He lifted her shirt up a little and kissed her stomach, tickling her ribs with his tongue.

This didn't feel awkward or clumsy. This felt exciting and scary, hot and shivering. She hoped he would pull her shirt off, both relieved and disappointed when he didn't.

Slow... *mmm*... gentle... *mmm*.... Yes, that was the way to go... for now. She ran her hands under his shirt, tracing the lines of his muscles with her fingertips, smiling when he moaned.

"Trying to tickle *me* now?"

"Maybe just a little."

"Troublemaker." He laughed when her fingers floated over his ribs. "I gotta punish you for that."

"Oh!" she gasped, and her heart skipped at the flicker of pure mischief in his eyes. "Is that a good thing?"

He kissed her deeply. "No, It's a bad thing." He whispered on her lips, "So. Very. Bad." He pushed her shirt up over her bra and stroked her lace-covered nipples with his thumbs.

She squirmed beneath him. The lace did nothing to shield her from his touch. It actually added friction to the heat from his hands, and her body responded in a fevered rush. His hands caressed her breasts, but to her surprise and delight, she felt a hot wet throbbing pulse between her thighs. *Please please please touch there too.* She couldn't say the words, so she arched into his hands, her body begging for what her lips couldn't.

"Tell me what you want, Janie." He looked straight at her, as if he needed permission to continue.

How could she tell him what she wanted? She wanted to be naked under his hands. She wanted to feel his mouth on her bare skin, but she couldn't say the words. Not yet. "More," she whispered.

"More what?"

"More." She couldn't explain. "Bad things."

Austin laughed and unhooked her bra with one hand, pushing it out of his way. His mouth teased one nipple while his fingers stroked the other one. "So pretty, so soft, so much better than I imagined. So. Very. Good."

She forgot about feeling nervous. She forgot about feeling awkward. She forgot about everything except feeling his touch, his kiss, his flickering tongue. Her body ached all over, wanting more, needing more, especially the hot wet place between her legs. Could she tell him that? She didn't need to. His hand left her breast to stroke her thighs, sliding between them and up until he rubbed the place she needed him the most.

But her nipple needed him too. "I wish you had more hands," she groaned.

He grunted, as if his over-stimulated brain couldn't handle a clever reply. He kissed, and licked, and touched, and kissed her all over again. "Oh, Janie, you turn me on so much." He kissed her mouth, his tongue teasing hers.

She closed her eyes so he couldn't see her wondering how many other girls he'd said those same words to. It didn't matter. He was saying those words to her, and he was saying her name. He wanted *her*.

He lifted his head and stared down at her, catching his breath. "You're the most erotic thing I've ever seen. So damn sexy." He kept watching her face as he unbuttoned her jeans.

She held her breath as he eased the zipper down, and she opened her eyes.

"More?" His fingers tempted her vulnerable flesh.

"Yes."

He leaned over and kissed her, his hand sliding into her open jeans, caressing her hot skin. He sat back and peeked at the deep purple lace that matched her bra. "I approve."

She laughed and caught her breath as he caressed the long length of bare skin between her pushed-up bra and her open zipper. It was a lingering, deliciously thorough stroke—up, down, circling her nipples, reaching under her panties. He bent down and sucked her nipple into his mouth while his fingers searched under the lace between her legs.

"Ooohh." She let out a long, loud moan when he found what he was looking for.

"Like that?"

"Oh yes."

"No. It's, 'Oh hell yes'."

She giggled.

He pulled his fingers away. "Say it."

"Oh hell yes!"

"That's my girl." He kissed her and stroked her soft wet flesh. "I want you," he whispered into her mouth, then kissed her soft lips, her hard nipples, her quivering stomach. "You taste so good. I could spend all night nibbling on your yummy little body."

His mouth on her skin consumed her mind, and she barely heard a word he said. The things he was doing to her felt so.... She couldn't find the words, but it went way beyond good, way beyond wonderful. Could she do the same to him? She had to try. She reached for his belt buckle and fumbled with it. He tried to help her out, but he couldn't do much better.

"What's wrong with us?" Jane sat up to get a better angle on it.

Their fingers tangled as they struggled with it. "Got it." Austin kissed her.

Then they heard the doorknob turn.

Chapter 9

In one swift move, Austin pulled Jane's shirt down and threw a blanket over her as Sara opened the front door.

Her eyes narrowed when she looked at Austin. "What are *you* doing here?"

"What are you doing home?" Jane countered, zipping up her jeans.

"My sister and her husband had a fight so they came home early. I didn't feel like staying there while they were arguing, so I said goodnight to the kids and left." She looked at Austin and snarled. "If I'd known *you'd* be here, I would've stayed far away."

Austin took a step back, pulling Jane close as if he needed protection. Or was he trying to protect her?

"Austin, this is my roommate, Sara." Jane did her best to maintain some civility, but the other girl wasn't cooperating. "Sara, this is.... Apparently, you know who Austin is."

"Unfortunately."

"What did I do to deserve this?" Austin frowned. "Have we met?"

"Seriously?" Sara gasped, then turned on Jane. "I told you going out with him again was a bad idea."

"But I like bad ideas."

Jane sighed, and Austin laughed.

"I'm glad you think this is funny," Sara shot at him. "I'll be the one picking up the pieces when you're gone."

"Who says I'm gonna leave her?"

"Back off, Sara." Jane stepped between them. "I'm sorry I didn't tell you Austin was coming over tonight, but he's here now, so let's just try to be nice to each other."

"He doesn't deserve it."

"Wow." Austin took a step toward the door. "I know when I'm not welcome." He reached for Jane and took her hands. "I'd better say goodnight."

"No." Her body still throbbed. He had to be feeling it too.

"I'll see you tomorrow. We'll make other plans." He held her face in his hands and kissed her. "Thank you for dinner. It was delicious."

He pulled her close and pressed his lips to her ear. "And so was dessert."

She answered him with a smile.

"Sara, I'd like to say it was nice meeting you, but...." Austin winced.

Jane followed him to the door, whispered "Sweet dreams," and closed it behind him.

"Good night and good riddance," Sara growled. "I hope you're not planning on—"

"Don't you ever treat one of my friends that way again!" Jane advanced on Sara, her voice low. "Do you understand me?"

"So he's a friend now?"

"He's a better one than you are tonight."

"I'm trying to protect you."

"From what? From having a good time? From laughing, from kissing, from possibly having the best sex of my life?"

"From getting your heart broken."

"Okay. I get that. If I'm making a mistake, if I end up getting hurt, so be it. I can take care of myself."

"But you're not thinking straight. You're not thinking about the future. There *is* no future with him."

"I don't care about the future. All I care about is right now, and right now, I'm having a good time with Austin. I'll go out with him whenever I want, as often as I want. I don't need your protection."

"Fine, but don't come crying to me when he runs off with the next pretty thing." Sara stomped off to her room and slammed the door.

Jane dropped her head in her hands. Would she see Austin again? She wouldn't blame him if Sara had scared him off. She didn't know Sara could be that mean.

She sighed and sank down on the couch. Still warm from their body heat, it brought back not just memories of his touch, but all the sensations that went along with it. Her body started to throb again.

Maybe doing the dishes would help distract her. She went to the kitchen, smiling as she set the dishes on the counter where he'd kissed her and touched her thighs. Oh, she was distracted all right, but not the way she'd intended. Without thinking, she slipped her hand inside her shirt and brushed her fingers across her nipple. *Ooohhhh.* It felt much better when he touched her, but....

Oh, screw the dishes! She needed a stronger distraction.

She went to her room, locked the door, took off her clothes, and finished what Austin had started. She would welcome sleep with a smile.

***

"You look like you could use a beer."

Austin said, "I could use something a lot stronger than that." *Like a certain hot-blooded soccer goddess.*

Jack opened a bottle and handed it to him. Austin sat on the couch and downed half of it in one swallow.

"What happened?"

"Her roommate happened."

"That sucks. Roommates can be a real pain in the ass."

"Ya think?" Austin polished off his beer. "Sorry, man, I wasn't talking about you."

Jack got him another beer, but opened a bottle of water for himself. "I know."

"The woman hates me."

"Jane?"

"No, Sara."

"Why?"

"Beats the *hell* out of me." He shuddered. "And she looked like she *wanted* to."

"Gonna go out with her again?"

"Sara?"

"No, Jane."

"Oh. Yeah, definitely." Austin took a drink. "Sorry, my brain is shot."

"I can tell."

Why the hell am I thinking about Sara? He closed his eyes and called up the image of Jane at her door. Her eyes sparkled and her cheeks flushed a pretty pink. Her tousled hair spilled over her shoulders in all directions; her shirt and jeans fit nice and snug. And barefoot too. Very sexy. Very....

Damn it! Something else bothered him. Sara had said she'd be the one picking up the pieces when he left Jane, but right now, he couldn't imagine doing that to her. Most of his relationships didn't last through next Tuesday, but he couldn't see an end to this one yet. *Hm... do I like that or not?*

"So other than the psycho roommate, how was your night?"

"Great. She's an amazing cook, even better than my mother."

"Wow."

"Don't tell my mom I said that."

"Hey, if I lie to her, she won't feed me anymore."

"I got no problem with that. More for me."

"So how far did you get with her?"

"You're talking about Janie, right?"

"Yeah, dumbass."

Austin held up three fingers. "And then psycho roommate walked in on us."

"Oh, man, that had to hurt."

"Uh-huh."

"But anticipation can be a lot of fun."

"Anticipation makes you insane."

"That explains a lot."

"Yeah."

He'd never dealt with anticipation before. He couldn't wait to see her again, but not just because he wanted to finish what they'd started. No, he couldn't wait to talk with her and laugh with her. He wanted to argue with her some more. He'd fought with women before, but when Jane fought back, she challenged him and made him think. Fighting with her excited him... almost as much as foreplay.

Austin frowned and wondered if he should enjoy that as much as he had.

"You okay, man?"

He jumped. How did Jack know? The guy had a gift for reading people. "Yeah, I'm fine." He got up and headed to his bedroom. "I just gotta figure out how to get some sleep tonight."

"No running around the football field?"

"Nope. That's not gonna cut it."

"Do you want to talk about it?"

Austin looked back at his friend and laughed. "Jack, you're way too sensitive. Are you sure you're a guy?"

"Angie says so. You didn't answer my question."

"I don't even know what to talk about." Austin shut his bedroom door then opened it again. "That means no."

"I got it."

But before the latch clicked, he popped the door open again and spun back to the living room, pacing and snarling at Jack. "Why am I so...? Why can't I find the words?"

"Confused?"

"Yeah, that's one word." He plopped down on the couch and ripped his hands through his hair. "I promised Janie a good time—nothing more."

"But you want more."

"Yeah."

"And that scares the shit out of you."

He growled at Jack, but his friend wouldn't retreat. "I promised Natalie I'd wait for her to graduate."

"I remember."

"One year. I'd wait for her to join me here, and I swore I wouldn't see anyone else."

Jack nodded. "Shocked the hell out of me, but I knew you'd do your best."

"But she didn't care. My leaving for college wasn't the problem. She said my future was too uncertain. I had no plan. 'What if you get hurt and don't make it in the NFL? What will you do then?' I couldn't answer her."

"You can now."

"Yes, I can."

"So why is that keeping you from being with Jane?"

"It isn't. It's something else."

"You don't want to get hurt again."

"Stop reading my mind, Jack."

"I can read you like a freaking book. Want to know what I think?"

"You're gonna tell me, whether I want to or not."

"True. I think you might get hurt again."

"That's comforting."

"But I think you've gotta take the chance. Jane's worth it."

"I know *she* is." Austin looked straight into his best friend's eyes and saw his uncertain face mirrored back at him. "Am *I*?"

"You are, and you always have been. You got me through some pretty horrible shit when we were in high school. You're good enough for me. But if you don't believe that, Jane won't either." Jack punched Austin's shoulder and yawned. "Goodnight."

Austin sat on the couch until he couldn't keep his eyes open. Was he good enough for Janie? Maybe. Could he risk that rejection again?

He wasn't going to figure this out tonight, not with his body still revved-up and his brain spinning its wheels. He dragged his sorry ass to his room, undressed, and crawled into bed exhausted—completely drained, and not in a good way. Every time he closed his eyes, images of purple lace, pretty toes, and perky nipples bombarded him. Sweet dreams.

A goodnight blessing? No, a curse.

Sweet dreams, yes. Sleep, no.

***

Well then, she could wait and wish and hope Austin would find her, or she could go find him herself. So she did.

All day, Jane searched for Austin, but she never found him. They didn't have any classes together, and he never went to the library. Where would he be? *The football field, dummy.* Now that she thought about it, she'd only ever seen him around the gym and the athletic fields.

She got away from soccer practice as soon as she could and hurried over to the football field.

Austin spotted her right away. "Hey, Janie, go deep!" He launched the football at her.

Jane kept her eye on the ball, took two steps to her left, one step back, and caught it with ease.

"Nice moves." He jogged over to her.

She laughed. "I just came from soccer practice, so I had to resist the urge to kick it back to you."

"I'd love to see that." He lifted her face in his hands and touched his lips to hers—soft and gentle—promising more in the right time and place.

That kiss erased any doubt that Austin wanted to see her again. She didn't even mind that he'd kissed her in front of the entire football team. She'd said she didn't care what other people thought of her. *Start living up to it, Jane.* "I, um, came over here for a reason, but I can't remember what...."

She raised her lips for another kiss, and he responded without hesitating.

"You just can't get enough of me."

"Besides that."

Austin laughed.

"I wanted to apologize for Sara, for the way she treated you."

He nodded but didn't say anything.

"She's not usually that mean. I don't know why she doesn't want me going out with you."

"She's just looking out for you." He shrugged, but avoided her eyes.

"Not the first overprotective friend you've pissed off?"

His smile held a tinge of remorse. "It's the price I pay for choosing to play the field."

She decided to let that go. "I told her I could take care of myself."

"You don't need to."

"Yeah, because if you do hurt me, I'll kick your ass through the goal posts."

His eyes turned playful again. "You can try."

"Don't tempt me." *Such a cute ass too.*

"Ah, Janie, I know so many ways to tempt you."

"I believe it." His standing there looking at her with those dangerous blue eyes was doing the trick quite well, thank you.

"Hell, I was awake all night thinking of ways to tempt you." He moved closer and ran his fingers through her hair. "And thinking of ways to make you give in."

Her heart beat faster. "Really?"

"I got no sleep at all. How about you?"

"I slept great." Her skin suddenly felt as if she'd stepped into an oven.

"Huh."

"After I... um...." *What am I saying? Do* not *tell him about that!* "Never mind."

Austin cocked an eyebrow. "After you what?"

"Nothing." She clapped her hand over her mouth to hide the naughty little smile coming on.

"After you took matters into your own hands...."

Jane shook her head, but her quick breath and hot face betrayed her dirty little secret.

"Why you little.... Do you have any idea how big a turn on that is?"

Is that just his cup or...?

"Was it good for you?" He gave her a sinful smile. "Too bad we're not alone, or I would definitely— "

"Hey Austin!"

"Kill someone." Austin swore, and shot a look at Jack that stopped him in his tracks.

"Oh, sorry, didn't mean to interrupt. Aaron and Greg want to know if we want to pitch in for pizza tonight."

"Sure. Sounds good. See you later."

Jack waited.

"I don't have any cash on me, so go away."

Jack shook his head. "Aren't you going to introduce me?" He winked at Jane.

"No."

"No class." Jack took Jane's hand and lifted it to his lips.

Austin rolled his eyes.

"I'm Jack, this idiot's roommate and lifelong friend. You must be— "

"Mine." Austin pulled her hand away from Jack.

She laughed. "I'm Jane. It's a pleasure meeting you, Jack."

A few inches shorter than Austin, he had broad shoulders and thick muscular legs. His blue eyes were playful and his dark brown hair a bit on the long side, but she liked it. Maybe Austin saw him as competition. He certainly could be.

"The pleasure is all mine." He turned to his roommate. "She's even prettier than you said. Be good to her or I might have to steal her away from you."

Austin laughed. "Good luck with that."

Jack leaned close to her, but not so close that Austin couldn't hear. "When you get tired of this guy, let me know." He winked at Austin. "I know how to treat a lady."

Austin pulled her close. "It's a good thing you're no lady or—Ouch!" He got an elbow to his ribs for that. "Jack, go away. Janie—" His eyes hid nothing. "—you need to be punished."

She caught her breath. His smile made her ache.

"I see you remember that."

"Okay, I am outta here." Jack slapped Austin between the shoulders.

"It's about time," he grumbled.

"Jane, nice meeting you. I'm sure I'll see more of you." Jack gave her a suggestive smile.

Austin stepped between them. "Not if I can help it."

"Do something about her knee, will ya? She's bleeding all over the place."

"Holy hell, Janie. What happened?"

All three of them looked at her right knee—bruised, swollen, and dripping blood all the way down to her cleats.

"Oh, I got kicked in practice. Soccer hazard."

"You just noticed that?" Jack cuffed Austin upside the head. "Some sports doc you're gonna be."

"I wasn't looking at her knees," Austin growled through his teeth. "Janie, sit down. Jack, get me a towel, a bandage, and an ice pack."

He helped Jane to the bleachers, then flexed her knee up and down, making sure nothing was broken, and that she had full range of motion. He wiped the blood with the towel and sent Jack for some soap and water.

"This will sting a little." He cleaned the dirt from the wound and wrapped her knee with the bandage.

A tear escaped her tightly closed eyes, but she didn't complain.

"Keep the ice on as long as you can. Walk on it, but don't put your full weight on your knee. Don't let it get stiff."

"Yes, doctor," she teased him.

"I mean it. You have to keep it moving if you don't want any permanent damage."

She laughed.

"What's funny? Did you get kicked in the head too?"

"I'm sorry. There's a dirty joke here somewhere about playing doctor with you." She wiped tears from her eyes. "This isn't quite how I imagined it."

"You won't be laughing when this thing wakes you up throbbing in the middle of the night."

They both laughed at that one.

"Believe me, I know." He winked. "All right, woman, get off your ass and try to walk."

Austin and Jack took her arms and helped her walk to the gym.

"It doesn't really hurt that much." She hadn't even noticed she was injured until Jack pointed it out.

"It will," the guys said in unison.

"I gotta hit the showers," Jack announced, breaking up the party. "I'll see you two later."

"Bye," Jane called after him. "I like him. He's a lot nicer than *my* roommate."

"Can't argue with that."

"So you're interested in sports medicine?"

"Yeah. I blew out my knee during a game freshman year, and Coach took me to a clinic specializing in athletic injuries. The doctors were amazing. They helped me recover fast enough to finish the season and start again the next year, but...." He looked at her, and then held her arm a little tighter. "I'll never play beyond college. I'll never make it to the NFL."

"I'm sorry." She put her arm around him.

Jane remembered that game. The whole school feared they'd lost their most promising quarterback, and everyone cheered when Austin came off the injured reserve list.

"I can't scramble like I used to. That's why I depend on my arm and a good running back like Jack. So when I had to figure out what else to do with my life, I decided I wanted to help other athletes like me."

She hadn't expected Austin to be the one with a plan, with goals, with a purpose. "And here I thought you stayed in school for the cheerleaders."

"Yeah, that's a definite perk." He leaned back against the gym wall, taking her in his arms. "I'm a pre-med major, so I don't spend all my time at the gym. I even go to class now and then."

"That's why we never see each other. I'm a business major."

"What kind of business?"

"I haven't decided." She had an idea, but she wasn't ready to tell anyone about it, so she changed the subject.

"So, have you changed your mind yet?"

Chapter 10

"About sleeping with you?" Austin nuzzled her neck. "Hell yes, first chance we get—"

"No!" Jane laughed and pushed him away. "Have you changed your mind about lo—" *Good lord, what am I asking him?* Her smile faded and she looked down at her bandaged knee. *Of course,* his first thought was about sex. What had she expected? "Forget I asked."

"No, I won't forget." He frowned, his blue eyes penetrating her. "Did you think you changed my mind already?"

She shrugged, not looking at him. "I hoped."

"Hope is a useless emotion too."

She stepped back and searched his face. "What made you so cynical?"

"Life did. Real life, Janie." His eyes narrowed. "There was this girl in high school...." He shook his head and started over. "The night my parents split up, my dad told my mom he loved her, but it didn't do any good. They still got divorced and they still hate each other."

"It doesn't have to be like that."

"Does anyone have a choice? Do I?"

"I believe we can choose to be happy." She looked into his doubting eyes, hoping he would see her confidence and believe it too.

He shook his head. "I'm glad you believe that, Janie, because I don't."

"What do you believe in?"

A wicked grin lit up his face as his gaze slid over her body, stripping her defenses. "Hot sex, cold beer, and the last-second Hail Mary pass."

But his grin faded all too quickly.

"I believe—I *know*—that dreams can be shattered in a moment." He took a determined step toward her. "I believe in taking what I want with both hands and never letting go."

He grabbed a fistful of her hair and pulled her head back, kissing her lips, her neck—whatever his mouth could reach—then slid his other hand down her back, grabbed a handful of her ass and pulled her up against him.

His passion and conviction thrilled her to the core. "Wow! I can't believe how much that turned me on." As quickly as it had started, their fight ended... for now.

Austin half-laughed, half-groaned, and turned her back against the wall. He slid both hands under her thighs, picked her up, and wrapped her legs around his waist, pinning her against the wall with his body.

Her knee throbbed, but she ignored it, focusing on the throbbing between her legs. She couldn't tell if the aching pulse came from her body or his. Didn't matter. It felt good either way.

"Tell me you want me." He whispered the words on her skin.

"I want you, Austin."

"Tell me what you want me to do to you." He rocked against her, imitating what he wanted to hear.

"Oh...." She bit her lip and shook her head.

"I know you want to."

She nodded.

"But you just can't say it."

"Not yet."

He kissed her, exploring her mouth with his tongue, teasing her with his lips. "I will hear you say it."

She saw the sparkle in his eyes and turned away. That devil was using her own words against her. Her heart pounded and her knee throbbed. "Ow!"

"That's not what I wanted to hear." He set her down gently, and put the ice pack back on her knee. "Sorry, Janie, I wasn't trying to get you so excited."

"Yes you were."

She pouted and he laughed.

"Damn right."

He kissed her lower lip and her heart started pounding again.

"That cute little pouty lip makes me wanna do things...."

"Ow!"

"Oh, sorry, I didn't mean to hurt you."

"You can make it up to me."

"Mmm... I will." His lips twisted into a grin and his laugh sounded like pure evil, pure sex. "But I can't tonight. I have an exam the day after tomorrow I gotta study for."

She raised her eyebrows and laughed. "Of all the excuses I imagined hearing from you, studying never even made the list."

"Hey, I'm a serious student... sometimes."

"I'll believe it when I see it."

"Yeah, whatever. I need to focus on this exam for the next couple of days, but after that you're fair game."

His gaze swept her body, making her tingle. She gathered her thoughts enough to continue their conversation, but struggled to put a sentence together. "What class is it for?"

It took him a while to answer, and when he did, an embarrassed smile screwed up his face. "Anatomy."

She laughed so hard her ribs hurt. "Anatomy? Aren't you already an expert?"

"You tell me."

Ooo. Jane stopped laughing and grabbed his jersey to pull him close. "Maybe I can help you study." She slid her hands down his chest.

"Believe me, I'd like nothing better." He pulled her wandering hands away from his shorts. "But you are too much of a damn distraction. Stop that."

"No."

"So you want to play dirty, is that it?" He stopped fighting her off and let her have what she wanted, moving close and trapping her hands against his thighs, waiting to see what she would do.

He was looking at her. She couldn't do *anything* while he was looking at her. She kissed him and, when he closed his eyes, hesitantly slid her hand between his thighs and up—cupping, rubbing.

Oh, he feels so good—hard, hot, and— Damn! My knee is throbbing again. "Ow." Jane pouted. Apparently she couldn't play his game.

"I think I should take you home so you can get some rest."

"That's not what I'm thinking."

"Oh, I know what *you're* thinking. Troublemaker!" He kissed her softly, slowly. "Come on." He pulled her away from the wall and swatted her ass. "Go change your clothes and meet me out front. I gotta get you off my hands so I can have some peace."

"Good luck with that." She stuck her tongue out at him as she disappeared into the locker room.

***

"Did you get kicked in practice again?" Sara dropped her backpack on the coffee table.

So Sara was speaking to her today. "Yeah. It didn't hurt much at the time, but it started bleeding all over, and that's when I felt it."

"Nice bandage job. Did you go to the clinic?" She sat down on the couch and inspected Jane's propped up leg.

"No, Austin did that."

"Huh."

"He's a pre-med major, sports medicine. After he hurt his knee, he decided he wanted to help other athletes."

"So he can play doctor."

"Yeah, well, he's pretty good at it." *Wait, that didn't come out right.*

Sara snorted.

"He brought me home and told me to put my leg up for a while."

"He didn't stay to give you some special treatment?"

She leaned back on the overstuffed chair surrounded by pillows, with her knee propped up on the coffee table. That counted. "He got me settled and warmed up some leftovers for me, but he had to go home and study."

"Austin studies? For what?"

Here it comes. "For an Anatomy exam."

Sara's eyebrows quirked.

"Yeah, I know. He should be an expert."

"I'm sure he's tired of hearing that joke."

"Yeah, probably."

Sara stood and picked up her backpack. "Do you need anything?"

Jane looked around. Austin had put everything she might need within reach. She'd claimed that he spoiled her, but with a charming smile, he'd insisted that he wanted to. She could get used to that. "No. I think I'm good."

"Okay. I'm going to my room to study. Yell if you need anything."

"How was your day?" Jane missed talking to her.

"Fine." Sara sat down again. "Good, actually. I got an A on my Psych paper."

"Cool."

Sara sat there for couple of minutes. "Are you going out with Austin again?"

Oh boy. "After his exam is over, but we haven't made any definite plans yet."

"I see."

Neither of them said anything for a while, so Jane picked up the TV remote and started flipping through the channels, not paying attention to anything. Then she put it down and looked at Sara. "I know you're just looking out for me, and I appreciate that."

Sara nodded. "I'm glad you're enjoying yourself."

"I am too. I won't invite him over here again if you don't want me to."

"No, that's okay. Just let me know when, so I don't have to be here."

"Okay."

Silence. Channel flipping.

Sara sighed and picked up her backpack. "Goodnight."

"Goodnight." Jane shifted in her comfortable chair, adjusting the pillows. Was it selfish being happy when Sara obviously wasn't? She shouldn't be having fun with her friend miserable. She picked up the remote.

Oh, why not? She threw the remote on the couch, out of her reach. *Is it my fault Sara doesn't like Austin?*

Sara had made her choice.

Jane chose to be happy, and she refused to feel guilty about it.

***

Jane spotted him leaving the lab as she was heading toward the library, but decided Austin was much more interesting than any book she needed.

He waved to her, and she fell into step beside him. "How was your exam?"

"Over. That's the best thing I can say about it."

"That bad, huh?"

Austin put his arm around her shoulders and pressed his lips to her hair. "It was tough, but I think I did all right."

"That's good."

"How's your knee?"

"Better. It doesn't hurt much when I walk on it."

"Good." He touched his lips to her ear. "Did it wake you up throbbing?"

She gave him an evil smile. "No, something else did."

He groaned. "Janie, you can't do that to me when we're in public."

"Sorry." She giggled.

"No, you're not."

"Okay, I'm not." She wanted to kiss him but too many people crowded the sidewalk, and they didn't need an audience for what she had in mind. "So what are your plans for tonight?"

"Jack and I are going out for burgers. Wanna come?"

"I don't want to intrude."

"Are you kidding? He's been begging me to have you over."

"Oh." *Wow. A guy is begging for my company? Nice.* "Okay, if you're sure he won't mind."

"He won't mind, trust me. But no flirting. It's not fair."

"Not fair to him or to you?"

"Yes." He grunted, then grinned and kissed her.

She followed him to his Jeep.

McGinley's Pub specialized in Irish food and beer, but they served beer from all over the world. Jane had once tried to count all the beer signs on the walls, but she'd given up. More signs and logos covered the walls on the second floor, where the pool tables attracted Bayfield students by the dozens.

When they arrived, Jack was already sitting at one of the dark wood tables, chatting up a pretty waitress. Austin said they practically lived there, and the waitresses knew them well. They knew Jack didn't drink, and that Austin did. They also knew that both of them liked to flirt, and they all loved flirting back.

"Hey, Jane, nice to see you." Jack stood up and pulled out a chair.

"Hi, Jack, how are you?"

"Can't complain."

Austin slid his chair next to Jane and ordered a couple of beers and another Coke for Jack. "Ready for the game this weekend?"

"You bet. I've been looking forward to it."

"Me too. Revenge games are always tough."

Jane picked up a menu. "Is this the game against State?"

"Yeah, we beat them in overtime last year." Austin read the entrée list over her shoulder.

"They were not happy," Jack said.

"You scored the winning touchdown." Jane turned to Jack, remembering that game. Sara had gone with her, and even though she didn't like football, she'd kept her eyes on Jack all night.

"That's right."

"I faked a pass and handed it off to Jack," Austin said. "The defense had no idea what was happening."

"No one knew I had the ball. I had an open lane to the end zone."

"We won't be able to pull that off again."

The waitress put their drinks on the table and smiled at Austin. He didn't seem to notice.

"We'll figure something out." Jack winked at the waitress, but she waited for a response from Austin.

"Maybe we should recruit Janie." Austin slid his chair closer, rubbing her thigh under the table.

The waitress grumbled and left.

"You're joking." Jane nearly choked on her beer.

Jack shook his head. "Not at all. Soccer players make great placekickers."

"Ryan's still on the soccer team, isn't he?" Austin asked.

"Yes." Jane's knee was suddenly throbbing. "He's the one who kicked me."

"You practice with the guys' team?" Austin touched her injured knee, and she pulled her leg away.

"Coach says it makes us tougher."

"Ouch," Jack cringed.

"And I thought *our* coach was mean," Austin said.

"He is," grumbled Jack. "Think your dad will be there?"

Austin's face darkened. "You know what I think."

"Your dad goes to your games?" Jane moved her leg closer to Austin, hoping he would touch her again.

He took the bait, stroking her thigh as if he needed comfort. "He says he'll be at every game."

"We make bets on whether or not he shows up." Jack took a drink of his Coke.

"I always bet no." Austin kept rubbing. "I win more often than he does."

"I'm sorry." Jane rubbed her sore knee against Austin's leg, knowing he hurt more than she did.

He didn't show it. "He always has some excuse, some drama. I stopped counting on him a long time ago. Let's get something to eat. I'm starving." Austin signaled the waitress and she bounced over to their table.

Jane rolled her eyes and looked at Jack, laughing at the spectacle. Did all women bounce around Austin? God, she hoped she didn't start bouncing.

"What can I do for you?" The waitress's gaze moved over the football star, leaving no doubt about what she wanted to do for him.

They ordered burgers and fries, and the waitress left, not bouncing anymore, because it was obvious that all Austin wanted was food and Jane.

Jack finished off his Coke. "So, Jane, how did you get interested in soccer?"

"My dad thought participating in team sports would be good for me, so he encouraged me to play soccer and softball. I was at practice more than home, which was probably better for me than anything else. It drove my mom crazy."

"Your mom hates sports?"

"Her mom hates anything fun." Austin's hand slid up around her waist, sneaking under her sweater to caress bare skin as he leaned in close and nibbled her ear.

Jane gasped and caught his hand. "Now I *know* she wouldn't like you."

He pulled her onto his lap and kissed her. "As long as *you* like me, I don't give a damn what your mom thinks."

She giggled and moved back to her chair, but let his hand continue wandering. She glanced at Jack and suddenly remembered their conversation. "My mom thought I should spend all my time studying."

Jack shrugged. "Nothing wrong with that."

"No—*all* my time studying."

"I see. No, that's not good."

"So I stood up to her, and my dad supported me. I told her she couldn't run my life. She told me I was a stubborn and willful child, but I joined the soccer team anyway."

Jack looked at Austin. "Wow. You could learn a thing or two from her."

He jerked his knee to one side, leaving Austin to kick the table.

"Ow! Damn it!" Austin rubbed his shin.

Jane didn't know what that was all about. "Anyway, at first I played soccer just to defy her, but I got to be pretty good at it, so I played all through high school and college."

"And your mom never approved?"

"No, but I'm used to that. She still forbids me to do anything fun, and sometimes I still feel guilty when I do."

"You have to get over that," said Austin. "I thought you told her she couldn't run your life."

"I did."

"Then why is she?"

"She doesn't anymore."

"She still tells you to spend all your time studying."

"I know, but the last time she called me, I told her I could get good grades and have fun *too*. And then I went out with you again."

"Good girl."

Jane giggled and cuddled closer to him. "No, that makes me a bad girl."

"I'll make you a bad girl." He kissed her and dragged her onto his lap again.

Jack interrupted. "When are you two gonna figure out you're good for each other?"

Chapter 11

Two sets of puzzled eyes turned on Jack. "Did I say that out loud?"

Austin and Jane laughed and kissed while the waitress brought their food.

She ignored them. Actually, she ignored Jane. "Let me know if you need anything else," she purred to Austin.

"Wow, she doesn't give up." Jane moved back to her seat and picked up the ketchup bottle, beating it harder than she needed to.

"Give up what?" Austin stole one of her fries.

"Flirting with you. You didn't notice?"

"Nope."

"Does this happen every time he goes out?" She asked Jack.

"Pretty much." Jack rescued the helpless ketchup bottle from her. "You'll get used to it."

"No." Austin frowned. "She shouldn't have to get used to it. That's just rude. I'm with Janie. I'm not interested in anyone else."

Jack raised his eyebrows. "Whoa. Seriously?"

He'd said exactly what Jane had been thinking. She decided not to say anything yet.

"I don't do two girls at a time."

"Just that once." This time he didn't move fast enough, and Austin's kick landed square on his shin.

"Yeah, seriously. I'm with Janie now. She's all I want." He leaned over and kissed her and stole another one of her fries.

She wanted to believe him, hoping that he only wanted her, not just for now but for.... The word *forever* didn't seem to fit, but she would take him as long as he wanted her.

She grabbed his hand. "Don't think I don't see what you're doing."

"Hmm?"

Oh, those *must be the innocent blue eyes that charmed his mother and sisters and every other woman he ever met. Not going to work on me.* "Stealing my fries." Yeah, they worked. She took his hand away from her plate and put it on her leg. "Keep your hands to yourself."

He laughed. "I couldn't if I wanted to." His hand slid up her thigh while he nibbled on her ear.

Jack suddenly got very interested in his food. "Mmm... good fries."

"Sorry, Janie," Austin whispered. "Tonight I will not keep my hands off you."

"Don't apologize." It would be so easy to fall for him. She should really be more careful, but her brain wasn't listening.

"Are you gonna eat those?" Jack pulled Austin's plate across the table.

"Yes, I am, damn it." Austin grabbed his plate back.

"Maybe we should behave while Jack is here," Jane whispered to Austin.

"Maybe we should make Jack go away."

"I heard that."

"Good." Austin pressed his lips to her ear. "I don't want to behave. Do you?" His hand slid between her thighs.

She shook her head. He tried to kiss her, but she pulled back, glancing at Jack.

"Just ignore me."

"Okay, Janie, I'll be good... for now." Austin leaned close one more time. "But as soon as I have you all to myself...."

He didn't need to finish that sentence. Under the table, his hands told her everything.

"Um—" Jane stood up. "Excuse me for just one minute." She disappeared toward the restrooms.

***

"Scared her off already?" Jack laughed.

"She'll be back. You need to get lost."

"Yeah, I know. Soon as I finish my fries."

"Don't come back till...."

"Till when?"

"I don't know. Just don't come back."

"What am I supposed to do all night?"

"I'm sure Angie will think of something."

"True." Jack reached for Austin's plate again. "Seriously, are you gonna eat those fries?"

"Take them." Austin pushed the plate across the table as if that would get rid of him faster. He kept watching for Jane.

"You're humming again."

"I don't hum."

Jack laughed. "Whatever." He finished Austin's fries and stood up. "Have a good night."

"Count on it." Austin's smile left no doubt that he planned on having a great night.

Jack headed toward the door then doubled back, looking concerned. "Austin."

"Do I have to throw you out?"

He seemed to hesitate. "Jane isn't like all your other girls. And she's definitely not like Natalie."

"I know. What does that mean?"

"I could tell you, but I think you need to figure it out on your own. Be good to her."

"I will."

Jack nodded and left.

***

Jane washed her hands and splashed cool water on her face, but her skin stayed hot. Her body ached and she felt a little lightheaded. Was she coming down with something? *Yes, idiot, but it's not a virus.*

There was no escaping him.

She sighed deeply, leaning on the bathroom counter. *Okay, get over your nerves.* She knew it wouldn't be awkward with him. A hot shiver ran down her spine upon remembering how she'd learned that. She took a deep breath, trying to convince herself this was right. She wanted this. She wanted him.

Uh-oh. Which bra and panties am I wearing? She peeked down the front of her shirt. Red satin. She felt good in those.

Her reflection stared back from the mirror—eyes bright, cheeks flushed.... Ready.

A mostly confident but slightly scared smile curved her lips. "Are *you* ready for *me*?"

***

Jack had disappeared by the time she got back to the table.

"We got ditched." Austin pulled a chair back and beckoned her.

"I'm sure he has better things to do."

He slid his arm across the back of her chair, caressing her shoulder. "So do we."

"I can imagine." She leaned into him and her hand fell to his thigh.

"Can you? Have you?" Her body said one thing, but her brain might say something else. He didn't want to risk going too far too soon.

"I have."

He would explore her imagination later. Right now, he wanted to tell her his evil plans for the rest of the evening. "Do you want to come home with me tonight, Janie?"

She nodded.

"Do you know what that means?"

She looked into his eyes and nodded again.

"Say it."

"Yes."

That was enough for him.

He nearly got a speeding ticket on the way home, but once they got to his apartment, he decided he didn't want to rush. They had all night, and he wanted to savor every minute of it.

***

Jane stood by the front door and scanned the room. The place looked like any guys' apartment, furnished with the necessities and not much else. A well-used couch slumped next to an equally worn recliner in front of a beat up coffee table that appeared to double as a footrest. The kitchen, unexpectedly neat and organized, separated two bedrooms decorated with football memorabilia. She couldn't tell which room Austin slept in, but suspected she'd find out soon enough.

"This is a nice place." She braced a shaky hand against the doorframe, willing her feet to take the first step.

"Thanks."

He took her hand and pulled her into the room, wrapping his strong arms around her and kissing her until the shaking stopped.

She loved the way he kissed her. If that was all he wanted to do to her all night— *Wait, no.* She wanted more than kissing. "Are we alone?"

"We better be." He picked up a football and threw it at Jack's closed door. Nothing happened. "We're alone."

She nodded and looked around again, rubbing her arms. *Standing in Austin Sinclair's apartment. Alone. With* him—*the baddest bad boy on campus. Now what?*

He answered as if he'd read her mind. "No more waiting. No interruptions." He held out his hand. "Are you ready for me, Janie?"

She took his hand. "Yes."

He pulled her into his arms again and kissed her, full body contact the way she liked it. He slid his hand into her hair and tipped her head back, exploring her mouth, thrusting with his tongue.

She hadn't known kissing could be so sexual, but Austin was an expert. He did things to her mouth she couldn't wait for him to do to her body. *Why wait?*

"I want to see your bedroom."

"There's not much to it, but I'll give you the guided tour." He led her to his room and closed the door behind them. "This is the door, but you don't need to know where that is." He jerked the curtains closed. "Windows. Not important."

Jane looked at the bed, but he seemed not to notice, walking past her to his desk.

"My desk... will not be used tonight... but wait...." He stopped and leaned on it, testing its strength. "Maybe it will."

He winked at her playfully, those sinful blue eyes suggesting things that made her quiver all over again.

He walked toward her, and backed her up against the foot of his bed. "And this," he put his hand on her chest and gave her a gentle push. "This is the bed."

She drew a sharp breath and fell back on the mattress. "I like your bed." She stretched out on it.

"I like it better with you in it." He fell on top of her, catching himself on his hands.

She wanted him to crush her. Jane wrapped her arms around his neck and pulled him down on top of her, raising her hips to rub against him.

"Whoa, Janie, slow down." Austin pulled up, gasping for breath.

"Why?" She pouted, hoping he couldn't resist that.

He groaned and crushed her into the mattress, kissing her breathless. "No need to rush." His whisper tickled her lips. "I want to enjoy you all night long, Janie."

She couldn't argue with that.

"The first thing I want to do is get you naked." A promising smile touched his lips. "But I'm in no hurry."

She groaned. "Tease."

"Damn right." He nibbled her neck, his hands sliding under the soft green sweater that matched her eyes. "This has to go." He pulled it over her head and tossed it on the floor, exposing the shiny red satin underneath.

He kissed her while she tugged at his shirt, and helped her pull it off and fling it onto the floor.

She stroked his bare chest, her gaze following her fingers as they explored his perfectly sculpted body—every curve, every angle, carved for her pleasure, to see and touch. *To kiss?* She lifted her head and pressed her lips to his chest, slipping her tongue out to taste him—salty and hot. He gasped when her fingers caught his nipple and her lips followed. Her teeth closed on him just enough to feel his pulse throb under her tongue.

Then her fingers touched his ribs, and he laughed. "Remember what happened the last time I tickled you?"

She looked up and trembled as she remembered his hands stroking under her lace panties. "Oh yes."

***

He flashed a wicked grin at her, unzipped her jeans, and yanked them down to her ankles.

She kicked off her shoes, and her jeans hit the wall with a satisfying slap.

Austin sat back on his knees and stared at her. Looking at her was like seeing a woman's body for the first time. She wasn't the first—not by a long shot—but he'd never seen beautiful until Janie. Her breasts, still covered in satin, rose and fell with every quick breath. Her thighs, squeezed tight between his, invited his touch. Her whole body begged for him. How could he refuse?

Oh God, he wanted her so much. Anticipation made him insane for her, and it felt so good.

He crawled on top of her and kissed her, groaning into her mouth as her hands caressed his back. They slid around him to his belt buckle, but she struggled with it again so she pulled his zipper down.

"Looking for trouble, are you?"

"Mm-hmm." She slid her hand into his jeans.

Breathing hard, Austin wrapped his arms around her and rolled over so she was sitting on top of him. If she touched him too much now, he was gonna lose it. He pushed her thighs apart until his erection fit nicely between them. She moaned and ground down on him.

"Yeah I think you found trouble, Janie." He closed his eyes and let her tease him, driving him right to the edge.

When he opened his eyes, he nearly lost control right then. The sight of her riding him in only her red-hot underwear made him ache to get inside her, but he wouldn't rush this. He pulled her down on his chest and kissed her deeply, unhooking her bra and sliding the straps off her shoulders. He sat up with her, his mouth catching her nipples, nipping and sucking as her bra came off, all the while warning himself not to look at her.

He couldn't look at her, but how could he not look at her?

He looked at her. *Oh God....*

***

She'd found something, all right. Trouble, maybe. Sin, probably. Raw sexual pleasure—oh hell yes. She twisted her hips, trying to feel as much of him as she could. He'd told her not to rush, and she was trying to be patient, but whoever had said patience was a virtue never had to deal with Austin Sinclair.

Jane's mouth fell open but she made no sound. Austin kissed her, drawing her tongue into his mouth, letting her enter him the way he would enter her. They fell back on the bed, Jane finally undoing his belt while he wrestled her panties off.

He rolled on top of her again, kissing her bare skin. She didn't feel naked until his eyes met hers and moved down her body. *Oh God, he can see everything.* He could see the scar from her appendix surgery, and that weird freckle under her left breast. He could see all her flaws, all her imperfections.

She crossed her arms over her breasts.

"No, don't do that." He pulled them away. "You're so beautiful."

She bit her lip.

"What's wrong?"

How does he know? "What makes you think something's wrong?"

"You bit your lower lip. You always do that when you're upset or nervous about something."

He noticed that? She hadn't even realized she did it. "I guess I'm nervous. My body isn't perfect." *Like your other girls' bodies must be,* she didn't say.

"Yes it is."

"Are you blind?"

He laughed. "Trust me, Janie, guys don't see what you call flaws. All we see is naked." His naughty blue eyes moved over her body again. "Naked is *goooood.*"

She smiled.

"We see fun places to kiss." His lips touched one end of the scar and softly followed it to the other end. "Mmm, this is cute." His mouth landed on that weird freckle, licking it until she laughed.

"Stop."

He kept his tongue right there and shook his head.

"That tickles. Stop!" She pouted when he lifted his head.

"Am I gonna hear that word from you again?"

"No."

"I better not hear that one either."

"Yes."

"Good girl." His mouth closed on her ribs and he nibbled hard.

She laughed and gasped for breath. "No no no—"

Austin growled.

"I mean—*pleeeeease*."

He wouldn't stop. He nibbled her ribs, her hip bone, even her good knee. She squealed and rolled across the bed. He chased her and she rolled right off the edge.

He grabbed for her as she fell. "Janie, are you okay?"

She groaned. The pile of their clothes had cushioned her fall, so she wasn't hurt, but when she looked up at Austin, she wanted to die. She'd landed on her back with her legs still on the bed, and he was staring down at her from between her knees with the most evil grin she'd ever seen on his face.

"Enjoying the view?"

"Oh, Janie, you have no idea...."

He caught her as she scrambled onto the bed, rolling with her, kissing, groping, getting tangled and twisted in all sorts of interesting ways.

"Why do you still have your pants on?"

"Beats the hell out of me." He grabbed one pant leg and she grabbed the other. They stripped him naked, and he tackled her, pinning her down and kissing her.

She closed her eyes and switched off all the nagging doubts and annoying voices in her head. The only thing she could do—the only thing she *wanted* to do—was feel. Feel Austin's long hard body on her soft one. Feel his fingers stroking her breasts, her belly, between her thighs. Feel his tongue licking her breasts, her belly, between her—

Oh! "Austin!"

"Like that?"

"Um...."

He frowned, and she noticed her teeth clamped down on her lower lip.

"Has no one ever done this to you before?"

"Um... well... no one has ever tried...."

"Damn it, what kind of jerks do you go out with?"

The kind who didn't care about pleasing her. "He was nice. He just didn't really know what he was doing."

"Lucky for you, I don't have that problem."

"I didn't know much either." Jane sighed. "I still don't."

A light went on in his eyes. "You've only been with one other guy." He lowered his head and kissed her quivering stomach. "And it wasn't much fun for you."

"It was quick and clumsy. I haven't had much practice since then."

"Doesn't matter. I've had enough practice for both of us." He slapped his hand over his face.

She didn't think about that. She wouldn't let his past get in the way of enjoying the present. "You know, if your mouth was... occupied... you wouldn't have to worry about saying things like that."

"I see your point."

He lowered his head and kissed her thighs, on the outside first, then over the top, then down inside. He did the same to the other one. She couldn't complain that they finished too quickly.

"Spread your legs." His words burned hot on her thigh.

Oh my God. Biggest. Turn-on. Ever. She lay there basking in the giddy sensation while Austin tried to move her thighs apart with his mouth. *Oops.* She'd forgotten to comply, then giggled and bent her knees to let him in.

He moaned as he licked her, drawing slow circles with his tongue, slipping inside just a little bit, teasing her. He stopped and looked up, and she wiggled her hips, her lips forming the word please.

His finger slid inside her, first one then two, twisting and curling. He put his other hand on her mound and pulled up, exposing the pulsing nub hidden there. He kissed it and she gasped. He licked it and she squealed. He kept licking it and she called out his name.

"Austin, Austin, Austin, Austin, Austin." She chanted under her breath. She understood the mechanics of oral sex, and liked the idea, but this was the first time she'd experienced it and— *Oh, what an experience!* Feeling his wet tongue on her wet flesh made her brain melt out her ears. She didn't know if she wanted to curl up or stretch out, reach for him or push him away. She became a blissed-out, tormented mass of helpless flesh.

Not her first orgasm, but by far the best.

Austin's persistent, relentless mouth took her places she could never have gone on her own. When she wanted to pull her legs together, he pushed them farther apart. When she begged him to stop, he pretended he didn't hear her.

When she confessed she couldn't take any more, he laughed. "I know exactly how much more you can take."

When she dug her fingernails into his shoulders and arched her back, he pushed her to the breaking point, sucking on that throbbing nub and bracing himself.

Jane cried out and nearly lifted him off the bed. "Oh God! More, more, more! Oh please, I can't take any more."

Austin didn't stop when she would have. He paused for a few seconds but then tested her, gently touching her with the tip of his tongue. When she didn't flinch, he kissed her wet pink flesh until she started to moan and twist.

"Come for me." He whispered the words on her hot skin, and she obeyed.

Her whole body shuddered, squeezing his fingers tight. She couldn't cry out. She had no words left.

Austin crawled on top of her, fitting his hard cock between her thighs, touching, but not entering her yet. She spread her legs without being told.

"Tell me you want me." He groaned, his voice rough.

"I want you, Austin." She moved her hips, begging for him.

But he wouldn't take her. "Tell me," he growled.

She looked at him, confused. "I don't know how."

He whispered a simple, primal, vulgar command in her ear.

Jane's heart pounded as she looked into his eyes and whispered the words back to him. "Fuck me, Austin."

***

He plunged into her hard, taking her breath away. *Oh God, she feels like pure bliss.*

He'd never used that word before. He'd never known what it meant until now. Hot, tight, wet, aching, clinging, holding, touching, kissing—all of it at once. He planted his knees and drove into her, holding her as tight and as close as he could. He never wanted to let go. *Oh God, I'm gonna come. No no no.*

He didn't want this night to be over. Not yet.

It didn't have to be. He would let her catch her breath, rest a few minutes, and then they could do it all over. *Oh hell yes.* Just the thought of having her again nearly pushed him over the edge.

He could feel her pulse pounding in her throat, so he kissed her there. He felt her heart hammer under her breast, so he kissed her there too.

She grabbed his shoulders with both hands and pulled at him, running her hands down his back as she molded his body to hers. She tightened around him, and he knew she would come soon—and hard. His body responded to her, and he groaned as he fought to hold back.

"Please, don't stop."

"Never." He promised to make it last, and he promised to make it so good. Of all the girls he'd ever been with, Janie was the only one he wanted to keep coming back for more.

***

Jane had expected pain, but it didn't hurt at all this time. Austin filled her, stretched her, took her body over. The first time she'd just wanted it to be done quickly. This time she didn't want it to end.

She wrapped her legs around his hips and pulled him in, arching her back and moving with him, not sure she was doing it right, but it felt right—hard and soft, aching and soothing, craving and satisfying.

Austin whispered instructions and encouragement in her ear. "Move with me. That's it. Mmm... just like that. Don't stop. You feel so good, Janie."

"Oh, Austin... please." She whimpered. Something eluded her, something more she needed, but she didn't know what, or how to ask for it, so she begged and hoped he understood.

"Janie." Austin leaned down and kissed her. He pushed her knees apart, spreading her legs wider. He slid his arm under her, lifting her hips as he pressed down, thrusting and grinding, harder each time. He held her against him, using his entire body to stroke her.

He understands. "Oh yes. More! Yes!"

That thing she needed—just beyond her reach. Close, so close she could almost touch it. It grabbed hold of her and shook her to the core. Heat burned through her body and chills shot down her spine.

She wrapped her body around him and held on tight. "Oh God, oh God, oh God, oh God, oh God."

***

Austin felt her release and then he did too, pounding into her, hoping he didn't hurt her. "Oh, Janie, I need you."

He didn't know what he said or why, only that being with her felt better than with any other girl. He liked it—no—he loved it. What did that mean? Fortunately, or maybe unfortunately, his brain shut off before he could think about that. His body took over, draining all of his strength and leaving him exhausted and satisfied in her arms.

Chapter 12

A feathery sigh tickled Jane's nipple, slow and steady. She opened her eyes and found Austin resting on her chest, breathing on her bare skin. She smiled and ran her fingers through his wild hair.

He smiled at her. "I was right."

"About what?"

"You were definitely worth waiting for."

She didn't wonder how many other girls he'd said that to. Rumor had it Austin never waited for anyone. "Thank you. That means a lot to me."

She wanted to stay, but she didn't know how to ask. Maybe if she tried to leave....

***

He rolled off her and pulled a blanket over them, cuddling close and kissing her. His brain still wasn't working right. He wanted to tell her how much she meant to him but meaningful words escaped him. "Me too." That would have to do for now.

They lay like that for a long time, kissing, touching, holding. He didn't know how to ask her to stay. He'd never asked anyone to stay, not even Natalie. *Just ask her, dumbass.*

"Where are my cloth— "

"Will you stay with me tonight?"

"What?"

"Leave them on the floor. They look better there anyway." Austin's dirty mind flickered to life. "I'm not finished with you yet."

"Oh really?"

"That was just the tip of the iceberg, just an initiation. You have a lot to learn, my sweet Janie."

"Is that right?"

Okay, brain, cooperate. "That's not what I meant. I still have a lot to teach you... um...."

Jane laughed and climbed on top of him. "Then I am your willing student. Show me everything you know." She leaned over and licked his nipple.

He sucked in his breath. "You seem to know a lot already." He grabbed a fistful of her hair at the back of her neck and pulled her down on his chest. "But I still have a few tricks up my sleeve."

He pulled her hair again, this time to expose her throat to his mouth. That one simple hold had her completely in his control... and at his mercy.

"Teach me."

Austin nibbled her neck. "That's lesson number one: a little restraint is a lot of fun." He bit her neck and held it, her pulse throbbing under his tongue.

"Lesson number two." He let go of her hair and shifted her so she sat upright, giving him a great view of her naked body. "All you have to do to get a guy's attention is show up naked and bring beer." Her pretty round breasts bounced when she laughed. "The beer is optional." *Especially when naked looks as good as you do.*

"So what you're saying is: men are easy."

"Uh-huh."

She twisted her hips, making his eyes roll back in his head. "What's my next lesson?"

Lesson? What lesson? Oh yeah. He flipped her on her back and fell between her spread legs. "Lesson number... whatever: a hard man is good to find." He rubbed his hard cock against her wet flesh.

"Mmm... you already taught me that."

"It's worth showing you again." He pushed her thighs apart and leaned in close, stroking his hard shaft against her. She moaned and arched, begging for more, but he held back. He slid inside her, giving her just the tip, waited there a moment, savoring her hot wet flesh, then pulled out.

"Please do."

He slid inside her, just enough to wet her for more. This time he watched her eyes roll back. "Lesson number... oh screw the numbers. Anticipation is a good thing." He pulled out.

She reached for him. "If you say so."

"You taught me that." He slipped back in, groaning as she pleaded for more.

"Did I now?"

Out. "Yes you did, you little tease." He slid in again, just barely—waiting, enjoying—and then he slid out.

"You're so cruel."

"You like it." He pressed forward just a bit, twisting his hips while she moaned.

She didn't deny it. She wrapped her legs around his waist and tried to pull him all the way in, but he resisted.

"I hope this is torturing you as much as it's torturing me." He laughed when she grunted.

He would give her what she wanted—and more—but he wanted to make her crazy for him first.

She twisted beneath him, making his blood boil. *Who am I kidding?*

He was crazy for *her.*

***

"Why are you smiling like that?" Jane studied his face. His usual naughtier-than-sin-itself smile looked different. Even his eyes looked strange—bright, shining... happy.

"Because I like you. I like your sweet lips." He leaned down and kissed her. "I like your sexy neck." He nipped it. "Mmm... I like your fat nipples." He sucked each one. "I like this cute freckle here." He kissed it. "I like your soft, soft skin." He planted kisses between her breasts all the way down her stomach to— "I like this yummy spot right here." He kissed the nub between her legs, already throbbing for him.

"I like that spot, too," she moaned.

"And I absolutely love being right here." He sank deep inside her and softly, slowly touched his lips to hers. She melted against him and he held her close, kissing her more deeply.

Love? She should've known she'd hear that word from him during sex, but she'd take what she could get. Jane sighed and wrapped her legs around him, holding him tight, prepared to keep him there all night, if she could.

"But first...." He abruptly pulled out, sitting back on his knees.

Jane sat up with him, protesting.

"But first...." He laughed. "I have plans for you."

"Ooo." Her protests went right out the window. "I'm all yours." When that happy smile returned to his face, she knew she'd meant that with her body and her heart.

"I want more of this." He slipped his hand between her legs, his fingers teasing her, making her hot and wet again.

"Have all you want." Jane closed her eyes and leaned back on her hands, offering him her body.

His fingers worked magic inside her, touching and rubbing. He had the amazing ability to give her exactly what she wanted and to make her want more. Could she do that to him?

She opened her eyes and leaned forward to kiss him, keeping his hand firmly tucked between her thighs. "Show me what you like."

"Mmm... as you wish." He sat down with his legs on either side of her, draping her thighs over his. Still stroking her, he took her hand and held it against his cock, showing her how to touch him. He let go of her hand and let her explore on her own.

Her fingers circled him with a feather-light touch.

"You don't have to be so gentle." Her grip tightened and he moaned. "Oh yeah. That's the way to do it."

She ran a firm hand over his shaft, listening to him catch his breath when she touched the soft warm head. It swelled in her palm, hot and hard. She looked down and saw his fingers sliding in and out of her, her fingers sliding up and down the length of him. Watching their mutual stroking made her insides flutter. What would it be like to taste him?

She put her free hand on his chest and pushed him back on the bed, kissing his lips, his neck, his chest. When she kissed his stomach, he moaned and she looked up at him.

He flung one arm over his eyes and a hopeful smile curved his lips. He stretched beneath her, unable to stroke her body anymore, but she didn't mind. His hand fisted in her hair, gently guiding her kisses down his body.

He held his breath as her kisses moved lower and lower. "Damn, Janie, that feels so good."

She smiled on his skin. She must be doing something right, because his muscles quivered under her lips as she licked them.

"Tease," he grunted.

Or did he say please? Either way, Jane knew what to do next.

She moved into a comfortable position over him and lowered her head, taking him into her mouth. The last time she gave without much success. The other guy demanded it from her, so she didn't enjoy it at all. But she *wanted* to do this for Austin, and he let her feel her way around him, sucking and licking, a little hesitant and awkward at first, but he responded as if he liked it.

She liked it too—making him squirm and groan. She liked the hot velvety feel of him under her tongue.

His hands pushed down on the back of her head, not demanding but guiding.

She opened her mouth and took him deeper, looking up at him as she did. He almost seemed to be in pain, moaning and twisting, but then she remembered reacting that way when he'd done it to her, so she didn't stop. She hoped it felt that good for him too.

***

Austin moaned while she had her way with him. He wrapped his hands in her hair, holding her head, hoping she wouldn't change her mind. He wouldn't complain if she did; didn't want to push her into anything she wasn't sure about.

Her soft hair brushed his thighs, almost tickling him, but what she did with her mouth felt so good, nothing could distract him. He got hotter, and harder—if possible—and her body turned hot and wet where she sat on him. Her hot mouth held him with a tight grip. Oh, he really hoped she wouldn't stop. *Give her some encouragement.*

"Don't stop," he groaned.

If she didn't stop, he would explode. If she did stop, he would die. Some choice. He was finished no matter what she did to him. He couldn't let it end so soon.

"Come here." He tugged at her hair and pulled her up.

"Did I do something wrong?"

Lost in her naked beauty, he forgot to answer her question.

"Austin?"

"Oh, Janie, you did everything right." He moved beneath her so she had to straddle his hips. "As good as that felt, I'd much rather have you like this." He lifted her up and brought her down around his hard cock.

"Mmm... can't argue with that."

She looked so pretty—hair spilling over her shoulders and just brushing her breasts, legs spread wide over him with his cock squeezed tight inside her. He wanted to burn that image in his brain forever.

***

He pulled her down and kissed her, wrapping his arms around her, his hands in her hair. Her tongue played with his, teasing and chasing, pulling away and following.

Jane sat still on top of him, and he didn't move either. Kissing him like that felt nice, but there had to be more to it. She broke their kiss and sat up. "Now what?"

"Hm?"

"What do we do now?" She had him where she wanted him, but wasn't exactly sure what to do with him.

"Do whatever you want, Janie. You're in charge." He laced his fingers behind his head and got comfortable.

Oh boy. She'd never been in that position before—literally—and caught herself biting her lip. *No. No need to be nervous.*

"Janie." He pushed his hands under her bottom and lifted her. "Ride me." He slid up into her then pulled her down with him. "Hard."

The man could do wicked things to her with just a few simple words. She copied his movements.

"That's it. You're in control."

If she wanted it faster, she would have to ride him faster. If she wanted it harder, she'd have to take him harder. She moved slowly but deliberately, grinding down on him until he groaned. She picked up the pace, watching him gasp, then she slowed down again, making him writhe beneath her. A slow burn started between her legs, spreading though her body.

She suddenly realized she controlled the power to pleasure them both, and that knowledge pleased her most of all.

"Having fun?" Austin groaned.

"Yes."

"Huh?"

"Oh hell yes!" She slid up, squeezing him tight inside her, then thrust down on him, taking her breath away. *Oh that's fun.* She slammed against him, driving him in deep. *Wow that felt good. Let's do that again. And again and again.*

Austin snarled and grabbed her hair, pulling her down for a hard kiss but leaving her hips under her control. He wrapped his arms around her waist to steady her, and she sat up. His eyes glazed over and he seemed to be just barely hanging on to reality.

She couldn't let him dangle like that. She had the power to push him over the edge along with her. Knowing that made her bold. "Do you like the way I ride you?"

He nodded, unable to speak.

Just one more push. "Do you like the way I fuck you?"

He growled and thrust up into her, knocking her onto his chest. He kissed her hard, holding her still while he pounded her, punishing her for making him lose his mind.

Her body spiraled out of control and her mind went right along with it. Pleasure took over, becoming her driving force. Everything else blended into a blissful blur.

He gently rolled Jane on her back, still holding her. "Did I hurt you?"

"No, but I think I'm going to be sore in the morning."

"Yeah, me too."

"Oh really?" She snuggled up close to him. "Our star quarterback got beat up by a girl?"

He kissed her. "Hey, you play dirty."

"You liked it."

"Damn right I did." He pulled the blankets over them. "I don't think I can move, so it looks like you're stuck here for the night."

"I'm not complaining." But she lifted her head and looked into his eyes. "Just promise me you'll take me home before my first class so I can change clothes. I can deal with some gossip, but I'm not ready for that rumor yet."

"I promise."

She kissed his cheek and laid her head on his shoulder. One warning thought slipped through her mind before she went to sleep: *Don't fall in love with him. Tomorrow he'll say goodbye.*

***

Jane stood in the shower and let the hot water soak into her aching muscles, wishing it would soak into her aching heart too.

Austin had brought her home in plenty of time to shower and change. He'd kissed her goodnight—or good morning—over and over, holding her close like he always did. But he didn't *say* goodnight—or good morning. He'd said goodbye. He hadn't called her Janie; he'd called her sweetheart. Any other girl would've been thrilled, but Jane knew he used nicknames when he couldn't remember real names. He hadn't said he'd see her tomorrow—or today. He'd just left her at the door and driven away, his goodbye kiss still fresh on her lips.

She pressed her forehead on the cold tile. It was always supposed to end like this. She'd expected it. So why did it feel like her heart was bleeding down the shower drain?

Enough already. She turned off the water and grabbed her towel. She'd said she would enjoy it while it lasted. A hot shiver ran down her spine and she sat down on the tub. Wow, had she ever enjoyed it. But now....

Austin had said goodbye. Time for her to get over him and move on. She wouldn't look for him today, and would never see him again. *Not. Gonna. Cry.*

The face staring back from the mirror wiped tears from her eyes.

Okay, maybe I'll cry just a little.

***

Holy hell, she could've killed me last night, but what a way to go! I can take it – oh God – maybe.

Austin shuddered as a picture of his Janie naked and riding him took over his mind. That woman made him want to do unnatural things, and not just dirty stuff. He wanted to hold her close and kiss her sweetly. *Weird.*

He'd held her all night, too tired to listen to his brain so he'd listened to his heart instead. He liked what it told him, and woke up with a happy smile on his face.

He poured a second cup of coffee as his roommate stumbled into the kitchen. "What's wrong with you?"

"Too much coffee." Jack yawned and rubbed his eyes. "Not enough sleep."

"You need to get laid, man." Always in a good mood after he got some, Austin wanted to bust out singing.

"Ya think?" Jack grumbled.

"Good sex—no—*great sex* cures everything."

Jack grunted and collapsed into a chair as Austin bounced into him again. "You're humming again."

"Again?" *What the hell is he talking about?*

"You always hum when you're happy."

"Not."

"I'm just glad you're not singing yet." Jack shuddered.

"I do not sing."

Jack leaned back in his chair, a smug smile twisting his lips. "You've fallen for her."

"What?" Austin slammed the fridge shut and spun around.

"Head over heels, off the deep end... hopeless. You've lost it, man."

"No way. I can't fall for her."

"Why not?"

"You know my history. You know what my parents put me through, how bad Natalie hurt me. You don't need to ask why."

"I'm not asking why. I want *you* to ask why."

"What the hell does that mean?"

"Why... can't... you... fall... for... her?" Jack emphasized each word as if trying to explain rocket science to a preschooler.

"Because I..." Austin started, mocking Jack's patronizing tone, but his words trailed off when all his old reasons didn't make sense anymore.

"My point exactly."

Austin shook his head. "It wasn't supposed to be like this. I didn't plan on...."

"You can't plan love."

Austin's stiffened. "This is not love. I am not in love with Janie, all right? I like her. I like being with her, but that's it."

"That's it?"

"That's what I said." He didn't believe it either.

"Good luck with that."

"Oh shit! What am I gonna do?"

"Hope. Less." Jack laughed as Austin landed in the chair across from him. "First, take it down a notch or four. It's embarrassing to watch."

Austin gave him the finger.

"Next, enjoy it. This doesn't happen to you every day."

"Yeah, you got that right. This doesn't happen to me... anymore."

Jack laughed.

"Seriously, what do I do?" Austin stood up and ran his hands through his hair. "It's fun now, but I don't wanna end up hurting her like my dad did to my mom. Or like Nat hurt— "

"It doesn't have to be like that."

"That's what Janie says. I want to believe her, but I just can't."

"I think you should."

He shook his head. "I grew up watching my father hurt women he claimed to love. I don't have any other example."

"I've had some good relationships. I managed not to hurt anyone... permanently. Use me as an example."

"Oh yeah—you—the guy who was up all night because he had too much coffee."

"Hey, I was with a woman last night."

"The waitress doesn't count."

"Not her."

"Who?"

Jack shook his head. "So tell me about *your* night."

"I brought her here and she asked for a tour." They'd never made it to the desk. *Next time.* "I took her to my bedroom...."

"And?"

"And I took her home an hour ago."

"Aw, man, you left out the good stuff."

"I don't want to do that to Janie." He felt the urge to protect her, and didn't want to share her, or what they had together, with anyone else. "That's just rude, man."

Still, he had to share the pure joy in his heart. *Joy in my heart?* "I thought that after I slept with her, I'd get bored and want someone new, but I didn't. I don't. I just want Janie. I didn't want to take her home this morning, but I promised her I would. I don't ever want to break a promise I make her."

"You spent the night with her?"

"Yeah. That was so awesome, holding her all night. It felt like she belonged there."

"You are in so much trouble."

"I know."

"I'm happy for you."

"So am I."

"Hopeless."

Jack darted out of the room before Austin could find something to throw at him.

Damn it. Is Janie changing my mind? Can I change?

For only the second time in his life, the idea of falling in love almost appealed to Austin. "Not hopeless." He poured a bowl of cereal. "Hopeful."

Chapter 13

Austin couldn't wait until after practice to see Janie, so he began searching the basement of the library. When he didn't find her, he scoured each floor and finally found her in the loft, hidden away in one of the many desk-cube clusters, her nose buried in a book. He sat down at the desk next to her.

She wore a blue sweater with a short skirt. Her boots showed a little bit of leg, but left the rest to his imagination—which went wild. She'd pulled her hair back in a sleek ponytail. Her glasses lay on the desktop, and she rubbed the bridge of her nose as though it hurt. Either she didn't like what she was reading, or something else was bothering her.

"I hear an orgasm—or six—is a great way to cure a headache."

Jane nearly jumped out of her seat. "Austin!"

"And I just happen to be the guy who can help you with that."

"Shhhh...." A couple students looked in their direction.

"Sorry." He lowered his voice.

"What are you doing here?"

"Looking for you. You're not an easy woman to find."

"Why?"

"You're never where I think you're gonna be. I swear the library keeps getting bigger. Did you know it has a loft?"

"Why are you looking for me?"

"Why not?" He leaned close and touched his lips to her ear. "I missed you."

Confusion crossed her eyes. "I missed you too."

"I knew I'd see you after practice, but I didn't want to wait that long. You're gonna have to draw me a map of this place because, damn, I'm lost."

"But I thought...." She rubbed her head again. "This morning you said...."

"Damn it, Janie, if you don't stop biting your lip, I'm gonna bite it for you." Not a bad idea, but first he had to find out what hurt her. "What did I say?"

"You called me sweetheart."

Oops. "I'm sorry. I forgot you don't like that."

"And you said goodbye."

"Yes, I said goodbye because I was going back home."

She blinked at him. "You didn't mean it?"

Is this a trick question? "Mean it how?"

"Goodbye, sweetheart, it was fun, but I forgot your name already. Next!" She blurted it all out, barely blinking back tears.

He flinched. "I did *not* say that."

"That's what I heard."

For once, he had no smart-assed reply. "Is that what people think of me?"

She nodded.

He didn't care what *other* people thought. "Is that what *you* think of me?" He used to be proud of his bad boy reputation, but seeing Janie's eyes like that was killing him.

"I didn't want to. I was hoping I'd be the exception. Wow, was that ever stupid. You said you'd never commit to one girl. I didn't want to believe you, but now I don't have a choice. You warned me, but I didn't listen."

When he didn't reply, she closed her book. "It's okay. We had fun. That's all you ever promised me." She stood up and started packing her bag.

He couldn't move. His heart pounded in an odd way, and the room felt cramped and hot. "No. It's not okay. Janie, I promised you I wouldn't disappoint you, and obviously I have."

"You didn't disappoint me, Austin. This is exactly what I expected from you."

No. I will not hurt my Janie. He stood up and put his hands on her shoulders, turning her to face him. She wouldn't look at him, so he lifted her chin and looked into her shiny, beautiful green eyes. "You are the exception."

She blinked, her lashes wet and spiky.

"I am *such* an idiot." He ran his hand over his face into his hair, yanking it by the roots. "I'm so sorry I didn't say the right things this morning. When I took you home, I...." *Didn't want to let you go... ever. Why can't I just say that?* "It was seven a.m. and my brain wasn't exactly working right."

A hint of a smile curved her lips. "It was six."

"See? You can't expect me to make sense that early in the morning." When she smiled again, he pulled her closer and lowered his voice. "Especially after what you did to me last night." He ran his hands down her back, sneaking them under her skirt.

"Stop!" She gasped, but put her arms around him and held him closer.

"Do you really want me to?" He lifted her onto the desk, pushing her skirt up past her knees.

She looked around at the vacated desks. "Don't ever stop."

"I promise." He kissed her and bent her back. His body told her what his lips couldn't. He would figure out a way to say it eventually, but he could take his time, now that she knew he only wanted her. "You do know that, don't you?"

"Know what?"

I have to say this *at least.* He stepped back and took her hands. "You're the only girl I want to go out with, for now." *Close but not quite.* "Right now, for as long as this lasts." *Damn it, Austin, get it right.* "Right now I don't want to be with anyone else but you." *Ever.* "Does that make sense?"

Something else nagged him, something he couldn't express, but his jumbled words would have to do for now.

Jane searched his eyes. "Just you and me, for as long as we can."

Yes. Exactly. He pulled her into his arms. It felt so good holding her. How could she think he didn't want her anymore? He'd wanted her from the moment he'd first seen her in the locker room, giving him that disapproving look that made him forget every other girl.

"My Janie." He kissed her and slipped his hands under her skirt again, caressing her soft skin. "Let's go someplace where I can pull that skirt up, pull those panties down, and make you come so hard...."

She moaned. "I can't. I have class in ten minutes." Her hands found their way under his shirt.

"Skip it." He kissed her neck, nipping at her skin.

"I wish I could, but I have to turn in my paper."

"After class."

"I have practice." She melted in his arms. "So do you."

"Damn it! Okay, let me walk you to class." He picked up her backpack.

"Such a gentleman."

"Ha. I'm no gentleman. I need a guide to get me out of this damn library."

She laughed and took the hand he offered.

"And I gotta get us out of here before I do something to you that'll get us kicked out of school."

"That sounds like fun."

"Janie, you have no idea...." But *he* did—lots of them.

"Show me."

"Tease! You already told me we don't have time."

"Oh yeah. Sorry."

"Unless you want a quickie." He dropped her bag and bent her back over the desk.

She giggled and moaned as he kissed her neck. He pushed her skirt up, nearly showing off her lacey panties right there in the library loft. Her body went stiff—like his cock.

"Actually, that's a bad idea." He pulled her up and adjusted her skirt, making her presentable. "I'd much rather take my time with you."

She sighed. "You sure know how to make a girl weak in the knees."

He picked up her bag and followed her out of the library. "You're lucky you can walk after what I did to you last night."

"No, *you* are."

He laughed. "Got that right."

"I'm surprised I made it through the day. I didn't get any sleep last night."

"Really? I slept great." Cuddled up next to her naked body, breathing her scent, her warmth warming him, he'd slept as if he were in heaven. He wished he could sleep with her every night.

"Your wandering hands kept me awake."

"I didn't hear any complaints."

"And you never will." She shoved him into a dark hallway. "I can't seem to keep my hands off you."

"Is there some reason why you should?" He let her hands explore his body.

"None that I can think of." She kept touching him, teasing him—sliding her fingers down his chest, tugging at the buttons on his shirt, pulling at his belt buckle.

If she kept that up, Austin would pin her to the wall with her legs wrapped around his waist.

"Are you sure you have to go to class? Just imagine... you and me up against the wall, my pants around my knees, your skirt shoved up to your ears."

"Mmm... maybe I could skip it today." She kissed him.

"But that only gives us an hour." Austin probed her mouth with his tongue, wishing he could do more. "That's not enough time."

"An hour isn't enough?"

"All of last night wasn't enough."

"At least you're not bored with me yet."

"How could I get bored with you?" He snatched her hand away from his zipper while chasing the other one away from his belt buckle again. "I can barely keep up with you."

When she started unbuttoning his shirt, he grabbed her wandering hands and held them still. "Come on. You need to get to class. Save that sexy pout for later." He kissed her, gently biting her lower lip. "After practice, you're all mine."

"I can't wait."

He slid his hand under her skirt one more time. "How's your headache now?"

"Mmm... I feel so much better." She leaned closer and brushed her lips against his ear, "In so many ways."

As she ran off to class, her skirt swaying behind her, Jack's warning echoed in Austin's head. He was in serious trouble. He could handle that, but he'd never experienced trouble like Jane Elliot.

***

"Austin!"

A deep, rich voice bellowed across the football field. Both Austin and Jack turned toward the bleachers and waved.

"Holy hell," Austin swore under his breath.

"I win." Jack grinned.

"Not yet you haven't. The game isn't until Saturday. He'll find some excuse to leave."

They walked over to the bleachers where Charles Sinclair Jr. waited. "Your arm looks good, Son, but if your pass protection doesn't hold up, you need to get out of the pocket quick. You never could run to your right very well."

"Thanks, Dad."

"Good to see you again, Jack." Charles shook his hand. "It's a good thing Austin has you to carry the offense."

It took a lot to piss Jack off, but Austin's father had a gift for it. "Austin is a great quarterback without me. You'd know that if you were here more often."

"Why are you here now, Dad? The game isn't till Saturday."

Charles ignored Jack. "I have some business in town tomorrow so I thought I'd drive up early, catch some of your practice, and stick around for the game."

"Great," Austin groaned. Out of the corner of his eye, he saw Jack mouthing the words 'I win.'

"Go take a shower and we'll go out for dinner. Would you like to come along, Jack?"

"No, thank you. I have a paper to write."

Austin knew that was a lie, but he didn't blame Jack for bailing out. Austin would too if he had a chance. He looked over toward the soccer field and saw an angel coming to his rescue. "I have plans tonight, Dad."

"Cancel them."

***

Even from a distance, Jane could guess whom Austin was talking to. He had the same build, the same confident stance, the same wild hair, and the same expressive eyes. But the older man didn't smile, and his eyes didn't play like Austin's did.

"Janie," Austin called her over. "I want you to meet my father, Charles Sinclair Jr. Dad, this is my girlfriend, Jane Elliot."

His girlfriend? Jane gave his father a strong, confident handshake, ignoring the 'girlfriend' part for now. "It's a pleasure to meet you, sir."

She took Austin's hand and laced her fingers with his, standing beside him straight and proud. His father could try to intimidate her, but he wouldn't succeed. She gave Charles her sweetest smile—maybe a little too sweet.

"Girlfriend...." Charles smiled politely, and raised an eyebrow at Austin.

"That's right." Austin squeezed Janie's hand.

"Interesting."

When his harsh eyes swept over her, Jane shuddered, knowing how she must look—sweaty, dirty, legs bruised and battered, hair in wild knots. She thought about apologizing for her appearance, but something told her not to.

"I planned to take my son out for dinner tonight." Charles made no effort to include her. "I'm sure you understand."

Jane knew disapproval when she saw it. She kept that sweet smile pasted to her lips. "Of course, you need to spend some time with your son." She didn't mean to say it so pointedly, but maybe he got the message.

"If you'll excuse me." Charles dismissed her with a nod and turned his back. "Austin."

"Be right there." Austin watched his father walk away, then turned and pulled her close. "You look beautiful."

He was trying to soften his father's harsh assessment, and she loved him for it. "Sweet talker."

"I'm so sorry about this. I had no idea he was gonna show up tonight."

"It's okay. You need to spend some time with him."

"If you say so," he grumbled. "Thank you for understanding."

She kissed him. "I expect you to make this up to me."

His blue eyes promised all sorts of naughty compensation. "Count on it."

"Come to my game tomorrow afternoon and afterward we'll do something fun."

"I'll be there."

"Austin!" His father bellowed from across the field.

"Gotta go." He kissed her and took off after his father.

Jack stepped up and put his hand on her rigid shoulder. "Better relax, girl, or you're gonna blow a gasket."

Jane slowly let out her breath, watching Austin's father lecture him. "Wow. I didn't know Austin could be so... obedient."

"Yeah, his dad has that effect on people."

"Are you afraid of him, too?"

"No, I am not." Jack's jaw clenched. "That guy pisses me off to no end."

His cheek twitched and she caught a glimpse of a darker Jack she hadn't known existed. She wondered if he was afraid of anyone. "You didn't get invited to dinner?"

"Oh, I was invited, if you want to call it that, but I made up an excuse."

"You made up an excuse? The nicest guy on the planet... lied?" Maybe he wasn't as harmless as he looked.

"Shh... our little secret." The mild-mannered Jack winked at her, all signs of that buried anger gone.

She laughed. "Why didn't you go along and help Austin out?"

"I tried that once. It was not pretty. After that, Austin told me it was okay if I suddenly had something else to do."

"Lucky you." She packed up her duffle bag and headed toward the gym.

Jack fell in step beside her. "You got that right."

"How long have you and Austin known each other?"

"Forever. Since grade school."

"Has his father always been...?"

"An asshole? Oh yeah."

"And has Austin always followed his father's orders?"

"Pretty much. For years, I've been telling him he needs to stand up to his father, but he won't listen to me. Maybe he needs to hear it from someone else."

"Maybe."

"I don't have any plans for the evening, and I'm not in the mood to study. Wanna go to McGinley's and get something to eat? I'd like to get to know you better."

Jane giggled.

"That sounded like a come-on, didn't it?"

"No, you sounded completely sincere, but if Austin said it...."

He laughed. "Yeah, Austin has a way with words."

"Among other things." A tiny smile touched her lips and her cheeks turned hot. "Let me get changed, and I'll meet you back here." She trotted off to the locker room.

Jack nodded. "Sounds good."

When they were both showered and dressed, Jack drove them over to the bar. The bouncy waitress smiled when she saw Jack. "Hey, sweetie. Where's Austin?"

"He had other plans."

"Too bad," she pouted, and took their order. "Tell him I said hi."

"Sure thing, sweetheart," Jack's gaze wandered over her figure.

Jane shook her head. Austin and Jack must have been separated at birth.

They talked about the game until the waitress served their food. "So tell me...." Jane rearranged her burger, removing the onion and inspecting the tomato before taking a bite. "Why do women find Austin so appealing?"

"You should know that better than I do."

"Yeah, but I don't get it completely."

"Austin loves women, and he's not ashamed of it. They know he's only interested in sex, but women like men who understand that they're sexual creatures too."

Jane blushed when she realized Jack was right. Austin stirred her sexual nature, and she couldn't resist that. "Yeah, I like it."

"But Austin isn't relationship material, so every girl thinks she's gonna be the one to change him."

"I don't want to change him," she insisted. *Or do I?* She'd told Austin she wanted to change how he felt about love, but would that change him? "I like him just the way he is."

"That's one reason you're still around."

"Really? Tell me more."

Jack laced his fingers behind his head and leaned back in his chair.

"You have something he wants."

"Which is?"

A slow easy smile touched his lips. "When Austin figures that out, you'll be the first to know."

She rolled her eyes. "You don't know, either."

"I have a pretty good idea. His parents' divorce really hurt him, and his father's many marriages and affairs gave Austin a twisted view of relationships."

"Tell me something I don't know. He mentioned a girl in high school."

"What about her?"

"I don't know. That's all he said. I thought you might know more."

"I do, but obviously he's not ready to tell you."

"She hurt him." Jane searched for confirmation in Jack's eyes, but he gave away nothing, so she tossed the bait out again. "She still hurts him. Does he want her back?"

"No."

He didn't volunteer any more information, so she let it drop. "There must be something you can share with me."

He leaned forward, resting his elbows on the table. "Austin doesn't know how to deal with pain. He can handle physical pain. I've seen him get hit by linebackers all day long, and he always comes back for more. But he can't handle emotional pain—or emotions—at all. He'll run away every time."

"Running away doesn't solve problems."

"You and I know that, but Austin grew up watching his father do the same damn thing."

"Why doesn't Austin talk to his father? They might be able to help each other."

"Austin doesn't talk to his father—or anyone—about anything. Sometimes I can get him to open up, but not until he wants to."

"But you must know something."

"I know plenty, and I know that Austin wants me to keep his secrets."

She scowled at him.

Jack chuckled. "I see why Austin calls you stubborn, but I think it's your inner strength that draws him to you."

She didn't know she had any inner strength. Sometimes she struggled to make it through the day—arguing with her mother, grieving for her father, studying for exams, writing papers, and now fighting with Sara and dating Austin on top of all that. It took all her willpower to get out of bed in the morning, but she didn't know any other way. "Stubborn, huh?"

"Drives him crazy, but he loves it." Jack laughed. "I love watching him fight his feelings for you. It's very entertaining."

Austin had feelings.... Austin had feelings... for her? This from the man who'd just told her that Austin didn't know how to deal with his feelings. That explained a lot, but it made her head spin, so she deliberately set that new information aside.

Jack finished off his French fries and eyed her half-full plate. "Are you gonna eat those?"

She pushed her plate over to him.

"Can't let good fries go to waste."

"I see why you and Austin get along so well. You both indulge your guilty pleasures without a second thought."

"Men don't have guilty pleasures. If we like something—or someone—we enjoy it. Guilt is wasted energy."

"Where did you learn that?"

He shrugged. "That's just the way it is."

"I wish it was that simple."

Jack made sure no fries escaped him. "Why do you find Austin so appealing?"

She bit her lower lip. "He's just so sexy."

"So I've heard."

"He's fun, charming, a little bit bad...." *More than a little bit.* Her cheeks flushed hot as she struggled to meet Jack's eyes. "You probably know all that."

His easy smile lit up his eyes. "I've heard it all before." He focused on her, as if trying to look deep inside to see what she was holding back. "Somehow I don't think that's enough for you."

"You're right. It isn't." She didn't know how to explain it.

"You know what I think?"

"I'd like to."

"Austin has something you want."

"And that is?"

"Freedom. He does what he wants, when he wants, and he doesn't give a damn what anyone else thinks about it."

"Except when his father is around."

He chuckled. "Except when his father is around. Other than that, Austin enjoys life without guilt. I think you envy that." Then he shrugged. "But I could be completely wrong. Just ignore me."

"No, you're more right than you know."

Life without guilt. That's what Jane craved. Austin didn't feel guilty about anything, especially when he should, according to her mother's rules. And yes, Jane did want that freedom. Could Austin show her how to achieve it?

"So how do I get Austin to give me what I want?"

Jack laughed and his deep blue eyes sparkled, just as Austin's did whenever he thought something naughty.

"You know what I mean," she grumbled.

"Sorry, couldn't help it. That's for you to figure out. I can't help you there."

"Can't or won't?"

"You're very perceptive. If I told you how to figure out Austin, you'd get bored with him."

"I don't think that'll ever happen."

"Yeah, that's one thing I've never heard girls complain about. Austin's never dull."

She wanted to get more information about Austin, but Jack wouldn't cooperate, so she changed the subject. "Tell me something I don't know about you."

He crossed his arms over his chest and leaned back in his chair. "What do you want to know?"

"How did you meet Austin?" She cringed. Even though she'd asked about Jack, she couldn't stay away from Austin.

He relaxed and leaned across the table. "Third grade recess. Austin and another kid were picking football teams. I was the new kid in school, kinda shy—"

"*You* were shy?"

"Yeah, can you believe that? Scrawny too—looked like a stiff breeze would knock me over—so he picked me last. We fell behind by a touchdown, and I told Austin to give me the ball. He looked at me like I was crazy, but I plowed through the defense and scored. We've been pretty much inseparable ever since."

"I knew it would involve football."

"Football is our life. Always has been."

"Are you guys interested in anything else?"

"Girls." He winked.

She rolled her eyes and Jack laughed.

"We do have other interests."

She had to ask, because he certainly wouldn't volunteer information. "Such as?"

"After Austin got hurt, he suddenly got interested in helping other people. I'd never seen that in him before."

"And you? What's your major?"

"Secondary education with a minor in psychology."

"What will you do with that?"

"Guidance counselor or maybe a coach. I haven't decided what I want to be when I grow up."

Odd. "But Austin has. I expected the opposite."

"Austin isn't as superficial as he appears."

"I've noticed that." And that, too, was very appealing.

Jack looked over his shoulder, and then leaned close, speaking in a low voice. "He needs to know he's good enough."

"Good enough? Does he think his reputation scares me?"

"No. Never mind. I've said too much." He sat back, a closed book again.

She raised an eyebrow, puzzling over the secrets these two men shared. She couldn't resist a good mystery.

Oh, and speaking of appealing.... "Have you ever noticed that he hums when he's happy?"

"Noticed? It drives me up the freaking wall. He's been doing it constantly since he met you."

"It's so cute. He even sings a few words."

"Badly."

"They don't make any sense at all, but that's why it's so cute."

"Are you kidding me?" Jack slapped his hand over his eyes.

Jane knew she was babbling like a giddy teenager with her first crush, but she couldn't help it. Happy to have someone share her interest in Austin instead of judging her, she would enjoy it as long as Jack listened.

Chapter 14

Austin picked at his food. Usually a good steak and a good beer made him happy, but happiness was pretty much impossible in his father's company. He'd much rather be with Janie. Hell, he'd much rather be with anyone than with his father.

Charles picked up his knife and fork and attacked his steak. "Where did you meet this... Jean?"

"Jane, Dad, her name is Jane." Austin's baked potato let out a steamy hiss when he stabbed it. "I met her...." He remembered that first encounter in the locker room. "I met her at school... after practice."

"What happened to that cute little cheerleader you were seeing?"

Which one? "I'm not interested in her anymore." That covered all of them.

Charles frowned. "I think this steak might be overdone." He winked at Austin but kept eating it like a starving man. "Who else are you interested in?"

"Only Janie." Austin took a deep drink of his beer. He didn't like the direction this conversation was taking.

"All right, who's next?"

"Maybe you keep a backup on the sidelines, but I don't." *Anymore.* Austin decided not to think about that too much. He just wanted to enjoy being with Janie.

"I know a girl who's perfect for you. She's beautiful, thin, knows her place...."

"Not interested, thanks."

"...not too bright, but she'll look good on your arm."

Austin picked up his glass, frowning when he found it empty. "Jane is beautiful. She's strong and smart—a challenge. She wouldn't go out with me until I found out her name. I can talk to her and... she listens to me."

"Uh-huh. Her glasses are hideous."

"I love her glasses. They're intelligent sexy."

"Stay away from that girl." Charles signaled the waitress. "Let me fix you up."

"No."

The waitress smiled at them. "May I help you, sir?"

Charles scowled. "I hope so. This steak is overcooked, the potato is undercooked and the bread is stale. I want a new plate, and I'm not paying for either one."

"Yes, sir." The waitress barley held on to her smile. "How is your dinner, sir?" she asked Austin.

Austin looked her over: beautiful, polished, professional—and close to tears. "Perfect." Austin ignored his father's glare. "May I have another beer, please?"

She smiled a little more easily. "Certainly, sir. I'm happy to help."

"Keep 'em coming," said Austin.

"I understand." She took his empty glass and Charles's nearly empty plate back to the kitchen.

"Thank you."

"Would it kill you to help me out a little?" Charles demanded.

"Would it kill you to be nice to her? Your dinner was fine."

"She didn't need to know that."

Austin shook his head.

"Anyway, this Jean—"

"Jane."

"—is no good for you. You need to be with someone who will improve your image."

"What's wrong with my image?" Wait, his father had managed to insult them both! "What's wrong with Janie?"

His father raised his eyebrows.

"Forget I asked."

"What I mean is, you need to go out with a woman better suited to your... future social status."

"Are you saying Janie's beneath me?"

"I didn't say that. You did."

"You asshole." Austin lowered his voice as the waitress appeared with his beer. "Jane has more class than both of us put together."

"I doubt that. Did you see the bruise on her knee? What kind of girl gets beat up like that?"

"A tough one." He loved how she looked after a hard practice—scruffy and tired. She looked like that after she'd spent the night with him, too. Just beautiful. "She plays soccer, Dad. She gets kicked sometimes."

He wondered what his father would think of Austin's 'social status' if he heard that Austin had treated her knee. He wasn't in the mood to find out.

"She's not good enough for you."

"Why are you being such a snob? You don't know anything about Janie."

"Do you?"

"I know enough. I know I—" *What? Love her?* He couldn't love her. He couldn't take that risk. Not again. "I know I care about her, and I won't let you treat her like trash."

"Fine. How many games have you won this season?"

Austin knew the subject was far from finished, but he went along with the temporary interruption. "If you made it to some of my games, you wouldn't have to ask me that."

"How many?"

"All of them."

The waitress brought Charles another plate, waiting for an opportunity to put it down, but he didn't acknowledge her. "Good. Have you talked to any sports agents?"

"A few."

"And?"

Only a few people knew the whole story: his mother, Jack, his coaches, and now Jane. Austin's father didn't know, and he wasn't ready for that conversation. It took all his strength to defend Jane, and he saved what he had left to continue that battle.

The waitress set Charles's plate on the table and waited for his approval.

"Aren't you going to thank her?"

Charles waved her away. "What did the agents say?"

"Not much."

"I'm surprised they're not showing more interest in you." He dug into his fresh meal. "I love the steaks here. Perfect every time."

He winked at his son, but Austin just rolled his eyes.

"Are you sure you're playing well enough? Are your wins solid or are they lucky?"

"They're solid wins, Dad. We have a good team this year."

"I hope so. They need to make you look good."

"I *am* good."

Charles sighed and put down his fork. "I know. I'm sorry. I'm just concerned about your future, Son. I want what's best for you, and will do whatever it takes to make sure you get it."

After listening to his father lie all his life, Austin knew when he was telling the truth. "I know, Dad."

"That includes finding a good woman for you. This Jean—"

"Jaaaane," Austin groaned.

"—isn't right for you. You're going to get bored with her."

"It hasn't happened yet."

"It will. You're just like me. You'll never be happy with just one woman. I know this girl, cute as a button...."

Austin waved his empty beer glass at the sympathetic waitress, bracing himself as his father rambled on about the right woman for him.

***

Jane wanted to spend the evening with Austin, but there was no way in hell she would spend it with his father, so instead, she breezed through her homework, straightened up the apartment, and was still left with a ton of time and energy.

What to do with the rest of her night? Bake something.

She flipped through the recipe file in her head as she looked through the pantry. Chocolate cake, caramel, Sara's toffee bar stash—Jane would replace those. *Almonds... almonds... please let there be almonds. Yes! Perfect.*

"Wow, something smells good." Sara sniffed the air as she came in the front door.

"That's the toasted almonds." Jane checked the oven timer and started crushing toffee bars.

"I love it when you bake." Sara put her books away and hurried back to the kitchen. "Special occasion?"

"No, I'm just bored." She gave Sara a few almonds, relieved to see her in a good mood.

Her roommate eyed the mountain of chocolate and caramel on the countertop. "Did something bad happen?"

"No. Why?"

"That's a therapeutic amount of chocolate."

"You can never have too much chocolate." Jane laughed, toffee flying across the countertop as she snapped a bar in half. "I'll get you some more when I go grocery shopping."

"I forgot I had these." Sara picked up a toffee bar. "When I saw all this chocolate lying around, I thought Austin had found someone else."

Okay, that shouldn't bother me. Jane might think the same thing if the situation were reversed. She stirred the caramel sauce.

But it did bother her. Why couldn't Sara—or anyone else, for that matter—give Austin the benefit of the doubt? "Why would you think that?"

Sara's lips formed a hard line. "Because that's what he does."

"No. Austin doesn't cheat."

The toffee bar in Sara's hand snapped in half. "Is that what he told you? Where is he tonight? Why are you home alone raiding my chocolate stash—"

"I'll get you more tomorrow."

"—when he's out doing God knows what—"

"He's having dinner with his father, so I—"

"—to God knows who—"

"Sara, calm down."

"—while you're waiting to see if he'll come back to you?"

"Sara, I—"

Jane forgot her argument when she saw her best friend's red face, and the throbbing vein in her temple. The toffee bar lay crumbled in tiny pieces at Sara's feet. This went way beyond not liking Austin's reputation.

Realization dawned on her. "What did he do to you?"

"He... hurt... me," Sara ground out between clenched teeth. She snatched her keys off the coffee table and ran out the door, slamming it so hard a picture fell off the wall.

The oven timer beeped, but Jane didn't hear it. Too many questions pulled her focus. How had Austin hurt Sara? Did he really not remember her? Was he lying about not cheating? Was he lying about everything?

***

After escaping the torturous dinner with his father, Austin flagged a cab home. Halfway there, he changed his mind and told the driver to take him to McGinley's. He needed to unwind before he could go to sleep. A good beer should've helped, but it sat on the bar in front of him, untouched.

"Would you like some company?" A sexy brunette sat down next to him, flipping her long hair over her shoulders as she coyly looked him over.

"Sure." It couldn't hurt to let her sit by him, could it?

She ordered two new beers.

Austin thanked her and took a drink. *Much better.* Maybe he did need some company. He relaxed a bit. "I'm Austin Sinclair."

"I know."

"And you are?"

"Available."

He forced a smile. Normally a come-on like that would make him hard as a rock, but tonight he was uncomfortable for a different reason. More beer.

Her gaze roamed his body. "My name is Ava."

"Pleasure to meet you, Ava."

"What are you doing here all alone, Austin?"

"I needed a drink." Whenever he went to a bar alone, he never went home alone—but again, tonight was different. "I had a rough night."

"Already?"

"Yeah." He chuckled. "You don't want to know."

"Hmm... I think I can fix that."

A sexy woman like her could quickly make a man forget all his troubles, probably forget his own name too. Ava's hand stroked his arm and he pictured those long fingers wrapped around his cock. That made him hard.

She leaned closer, giving him a tempting look down her blouse. Gorgeous breasts, long legs, luscious lips—everything he looked for in a woman—his for the taking. So why didn't he just take it?

"I should get going." He tried to stand up, but she grabbed his arm and pulled him close.

"So soon? I was hoping to spend some more time with you, Austin."

Oh, what the hell. He couldn't let a good beer go to waste.

She moved closer to him when he sat back down, resting a hand on his thigh. He should have moved away from her, but he didn't. Her heat hit him, and she smelled so good, like a hot soapy shower after sex.

"So tell me...." Ava's hand moved up his thigh. "How would you like to spend the rest of your night?"

With Janie. That thought flashed into his mind before anything else could, leaving him unable to speak. "Um...."

Her knees parted, sending her skirt scooting up her bare thighs. Austin looked down and watched his own hand touch her skin, and just like that, he forgot all about Janie.

"I'd like to spend the night with you," she purred.

"That's what I figured."

"Interested?"

"Hell yes." *Shit!* Did he say that out loud? "I mean...." Yes, he was interested. Any sane man would be. Ava tempted him, no doubt about that, but his Janie.... *Am I insane?*

She waited, but not for long. "Come back to my place." She leaned into his body and kissed him hard. Her tongue slid against his lips and parted them.

Before Austin could reply, he pushed her away. "I can't."

"Why not?"

He wouldn't cheat on Janie. Another reason pestered him—lots of other reasons. "I gotta take care of something first."

"All right." She programmed her name and phone number into his cell phone. "Call me when you want me." She blew him a kiss and left.

Oh, he wanted her. For a second, he entertained the temptation to take her to the nearest dark corner and show her exactly how much he wanted her, but when he closed his eyes, it was Janie's face he saw, Janie's body he touched.

Austin stuck his phone in his pocket and walked out of the bar. *Damn it. What is wrong with me?*

Janie was the most fascinating girl he'd ever met. He couldn't stop thinking about her, couldn't stop wanting her, but as soon as a beautiful stranger in a bar kissed him, he nearly threw away everything he had with Janie for a night of meaningless sex. Maybe his father was right. Maybe Austin would never be happy with just one woman. He would get bored eventually—he always did.

He would end up hurting Janie. What had happened in the bar tonight proved it. He cared about Janie—he really did—but he cared about her too much to see her get hurt.

Don't hurt a woman you love.... The words his mother had said to him, on that terrible night when his father left, echoed in his head. Only ten years old, and he'd decided that he'd never fall in love. The one time he had, he'd barely survived. Love caused too much pain.

He stood at the street corner and waited for the light to change, knowing Janie's apartment building stood three blocks away. He took a determined right turn.

Only one thing I can do. It was going to kill him, but he had to do it.

He knocked on the door, hoping to God Sara wasn't home. When Janie opened the door and yawned, he realized he'd woken her up. "Sorry. I didn't know how late it was."

"Austin." Jane blinked and rubbed her eyes. "Come in."

He stepped inside but didn't sit down. He wouldn't be staying long.

"How was dinner?"

"Fine." He didn't want to re-live that. "Janie, I—"

She wore a long baggy t-shirt and nothing else, but damn if she didn't look like sex on legs. Her nipples perked up under the thin cloth, and when she sat down, she crossed her legs, leaving very little to the imagination. Did she have any idea what she was doing to him? *What is it again? Oh. Yeah.*

"Janie, I came over to tell you...." How could he do this? *Just get it over with, Austin.* "I can't see you anymore."

"What?" She stared at him with wide eyes, fully awake now. "Why?"

"I'm not—"

Her pretty face crumpled. Her eyes sparkled with unshed tears and her smile disappeared.

God, how can I do this to her? He had to. He would hurt her even more if he didn't. "I'm not good enough for you, Janie."

"Don't say that."

"After dinner I went to McGinley's and I met a girl there."

Jane sucked in a sharp breath.

"Nothing happened... not much happened. She invited me to her place and when I said no, she gave me her phone number."

"You said no?"

He heard a note of hope in her voice, and it was gonna kill him to dash it, but he had to. "I don't cheat, Janie. I always break up with a girl before I go out with someone else." The hope faded from her eyes, and he forced himself to continue. "I'm just gonna end up breaking your heart. It's better to end it now before you get too attached."

Her eyes narrowed. "Is that what you think?"

"Yeah."

"You think you can just cut me loose and go on your merry way." She stood up and crossed her arms over her chest.

Damn, she covered up those pretty nipples. "It's not like that, I—"

"So what is it like?"

Oh shit, I've pissed her off good. "Will you let me finish?" Why was she mad at him? "I care about you too much to hurt you."

"Ha! You have a funny way of showing it."

What the hell? "I'm trying to do the right thing—"

"No you're not. You're trying to do the easy thing."

"Easy? You think this is *easy*?"

"Oh, yeah. A new pretty face comes along and you manage to say no, but instead of trying to make it work with me—the one you 'care so much' about—you run away."

"I cannot commit to one girl. I told you that. I'm just like my father."

"That's just an excuse."

"That's a fact."

"Bullshit!"

Austin took a step back and stared at her. He'd expected to deal with tears and pleading, but this? "I touched another woman tonight. I kissed her. Doesn't that prove that I'm a heartbreaker?"

Jane clenched her teeth so hard Austin thought her jaw would break. "Yeah, you're the heartbreaker, but I'll be damned if I'll let you add me to your list of conquests."

"I would never—"

"Get out!" She stalked across the room, driving him toward the door.

Austin backed up so fast he nearly tripped over his own feet. "Janie, wait—"

"Get out!" She pushed him out the door and slammed it shut.

That had not gone as planned. Austin shuffled out to the street and hailed a cab. He'd faced angry women before, but damn. His hands shook. Why was Janie so angry? He should never have told her he'd kissed Ava. *That's my mistake.* He sighed and fell back against the seat. He didn't want Janie to be angry with him, but he couldn't do anything about it now. It was over.

The cab turned down his street and he stepped out. When he reached into his pocket for some money, he found his cell phone. He looked up Ava's phone number and felt nothing, not even a remote interest in her. He deleted it, knowing immediately that he'd done something right that night.

Another name and number popped up: Brenda. He deleted that one too. Carrie—deleted. Gina—deleted. Hayley—deleted. He could have so many women. Why did he only want the one he couldn't have? Janie.... He saved her number. Jenna—deleted.

He crawled into bed alone that night. Was his father right? Would he ever be happy? Or was Janie right? Was that just an excuse?

He still didn't have any answers when his alarm went off in the morning.

Chapter 15

After she finished cursing Austin and throwing things at the front door, Jane went back to bed. *Why am I so angry?* He'd flirted with another woman, kissed her, put his hands on her body. That hurt, but when he just walked in and announced it was over, *that* was when she'd got pissed.

He hadn't even tried to work things out with her. He'd just expected her to let him go.

She couldn't let it end like this. She needed some control if she wanted to maintain her dignity.

An hour later, she heard the front door open and shut. For a moment she held her breath, her foolish heart hoping Austin had come back, but when she heard keys land on the coffee table, she knew it was Sara. Jane thought about getting up and talking to her—she missed that—but she didn't want Sara to know what Austin had done to her. Not yet.

She couldn't think of anyone else she could talk to, no one else she could trust. All alone in the dark, she curled up into a ball and pulled the blankets up to her chin, suddenly missing her dad. She didn't move, staring at the clock as the hours ticked by one minute at a time.

Without even thinking, she picked up her cell phone and dialed. "Hi, Mom."

"Jane? What time is it? Are you all right?"

She tried to answer but could only sob.

"What's wrong, Honey?"

She took a deep breath, then another, struggling to find the words. "Austin broke up with me." Saying it felt like a knife through her heart, sharp and stabbing.

"I'm so sorry. Why did he do it?"

"He said he didn't want to hurt me." The knife twisted deeper.

"Maybe it's for the best. Love can hurt."

"He keeps telling me that, but I don't want to believe him. I try to tell him that love should be easy, but he doesn't want to believe me either."

Her mother chuckled, and Jane wondered what was so funny. "Oh, Jane, you are just like your father."

"What's wrong with that?"

"Nothing. He was such an idealist, almost naïve. He believed that life was always wonderful and nothing bad would ever happen to us."

"I'm not like that."

"Where do you think you got the idea that love and life was supposed to be easy?"

Jane shrugged, and then remembered that her mother couldn't see her. "From Dad?"

"You and I have both been through some very hard things. You lost your father too young, and I lost my husband—but even before that, our life was hard. Your dad did his best not to let you know. Both of you chose to blissfully ignore life's difficulties and pretend everything was simple."

What? If their life was so hard, did that mean...? "But I thought you and Dad were happy together."

"We were, but we had to work at it. When we first got married, things were pretty tough, but we faced our problems together, and after a while life did get easier for us. It took a lot of effort to get there, though."

"Hm." Jane hadn't realized that her parents had needed to work at their relationship. They made it look easy. Why couldn't it be like that for her? "But I want it to be easy now."

She sobbed, not caring that she sounded like a whining child. The last few days had been such a struggle, and she just wanted to be done with it.

"I know you do, Honey, but you're stronger than you think." Her mother chuckled again. "When I think of all the times you fought against me, I'm amazed at your determination."

Did she have any left? Jane wiped her face on her blanket. She could barely gather the strength to speak. "I'm so tired, Mom."

"Get some sleep. You'll be able to think better after you get some rest."

"Okay."

"I'm glad you called me, Jane."

"Me too."

"I love you."

"Love you too, Mom."

She turned off the phone, unable to talk anymore tonight. Maybe Austin had been right: ending it now might be easier than fighting to stay with him. Why did she bother? She enjoyed the fun he brought to her life, but was that enough? Had he given up because they no longer had fun?

What had Jack said to her? *Your inner strength draws him to you.*

If Austin wasn't strong enough to keep them together, then she would have to be strong enough for both of them. He couldn't just walk out of her life. Actually, she'd pushed him out, but that was beside the point. He had to know why she'd been mad, and the sooner she told him, the better. If he still wanted out, she would say goodbye forever, but if he wanted her back....

It was a big risk, but she didn't have any other choice.

***

"You look like hell."

Austin grunted and struggled to open the refrigerator. "Where's the coffee?"

"Not in there." Jack poured him a cup and put it on the table. "Rough night?"

"Yeah." Austin slumped into a chair and sipped the hot coffee. Jack usually made good coffee, but it left a bitter taste in Austin's mouth this morning. "Yeah, it wasn't pretty."

"Your dad?"

"Uh-huh. And too much beer, hot girl at McGinley's.... Long story short, I broke up with Janie."

Jack's mug overflowed, scalding his hand. "Damn it! Why the hell did you do that?"

"I didn't want to hurt her."

"You think breaking up with her didn't hurt?" He grabbed a towel and attacked the spilled coffee.

Austin frowned. "No, it pissed her off."

"So you dumped her for some girl you met at McGinley's?"

"No. I turned the girl down. I ended it with Janie because I'm gonna break her heart if we stay together much longer."

"You are such an idiot."

"Thank you." Austin's coffee made it halfway to his lips. "Um... what?"

"Jane was the best thing that ever happened to you. Did you even try to work things out?"

He hadn't thought of that. "No."

"Moron."

"Hey, that's harsh."

"I'm just getting started." Jack grabbed the coffee pot and dumped it down the sink. "She was good for you. Why did you have to go and ruin it?"

"I did the right thing." Maybe if he said it out loud, he would believe it.

"No. You didn't." Jack swiped Austin's mug.

"I'm not done with that."

"You were happy with her."

"I'm happy with a lot of girls." But he hadn't known real happiness until he'd met Janie.

"You didn't know happiness until you met Jane."

How does Jack do that? "I know. I miss her already."

"Good. Keep missing her."

The pain he'd tried to hold off ripped through his heart. How could he make it stop hurting? He'd thought leaving Janie would do it, but now wondered if he'd made a terrible mistake. Being without her hurt much more than being with her. "I want her back."

"I'm not surprised."

"How do I get her back?"

"I don't know. You could charm your way out of this with any other girl, but Jane can see right through your BS."

"I know. I am *so* screwed."

"Sucks to be you."

Austin dropped his head in his hands and groaned.

***

Jane watched Austin from the edge of the football field. She stayed close to the bleachers, reasonably sure he couldn't see her. He threw a long pass down the field, way over Greg's head... again. Jack jogged over to Austin and smacked the side of his helmet. Jane couldn't make out his words, but she understood his tone. Austin stood with his hands on his hips, looking down at the ground and nodding.

"Hey Jane! Heads up!"

Jane covered her head with her arms and ducked.

Ryan laughed and trotted over to her. "Sorry. Couldn't resist."

She looked around, and when she figured out she wasn't the target of a wayward football, she scowled at Ryan. "I'm so glad I could amuse you."

"Lighten up, Jane. You looked like you needed a laugh."

She had to agree with him.

"How's the knee?"

"Better. Austin bandaged it up for me."

"Nice to have someone take care of you."

"Yeah, well... that's over." She sighed.

"I'm sorry. What did he do?"

"What do you think?" She looked at him over the top of her glasses.

"Dumbass." Ryan shook his head.

She looked toward the football field again and watched Austin fumble a handoff to Jack.

"I, ah...." Ryan fumbled his words. "Maybe this is too soon, but I...." His face turned red as he cast his eyes toward the ground.

Is he trying to ask me out?

"I wonder if you'd like to go out with me sometime."

Her eyes widened. She'd had no idea Ryan liked her. Maybe other guys liked her too. She needed to start paying attention. A loud cheer went up from the field as Austin's throw connected with a receiver. Jane watched him celebrate with his team and her heart flipped over.

It didn't matter if anyone else wanted her. She still wanted Austin. "It's too soon, Ryan."

He nodded. "That's what I figured. But hey, anytime you need a laugh...." He pretended to kick her.

She gave him a playful shove.

***

"What the hell is she doing with him?"

"Who is doing what with...?" Jack took off his helmet and followed Austin's furious gaze to the bleachers. "Ah."

"Holy hell. Look at her. She's laughing with him and touching him—"

"*You're* the one who dumped *her*."

"Last night! Even I don't move on that fast."

Jack threw his head back and laughed.

"Shut up." Austin chucked his helmet on the bench and stormed over to the bleachers where Jane was still giggling. Fortunately for Ryan, he made it to the locker room before Austin got to Jane.

"I can't believe you're doing this to me. In front of the whole damn team!"

Jane's mouth fell open and she stared at him. "Just what do you think I'm doing?"

Austin flung his arm toward Ryan. "You used all those lessons I taught you on him. Flirting with him, teasing him—"

"Are you kidding me? Ryan came over to ask about my knee."

"Yeah, right. Is that why you had your hands all over him?"

She scowled. "I gave him a little shove when he asked me out...."

"I knew it! As soon as I'm out of the picture, you run right to another guy."

"I did not—"

"How long has this been going on?"

"Has *what* been—"

"I'll bet you had him waiting on the sidelines—"

"Austin, I don't—"

"—ready to come in and take my place as soon as--

"Austin, are you listening to yourself?"

He closed his mouth and blinked. He'd heard this conversation before.

Jane's eyes narrowed. "This is exactly what you do to every girl you've ever gone out with."

"No, not that." He shook his head. His parents had gone through this exact fight every time his mom caught his dad cheating.

"Yes that. I am not going to stand here and let you accuse me of...." Her face turned red and her eyes burned right through him. "What were you thinking?"

He wasn't thinking. He couldn't. As soon as he'd seen her with someone else, he'd just reacted. "Janie, I want you back."

Her eyes widened. "Yeah, this is the way to do it."

"I don't know how to do it. I've never done this before." He reached for her, but she stepped back. "Please, Janie."

Her lips formed a hard line and she took off her glasses, pinching the bridge of her nose again like her head hurt. "We need to talk. Now."

***

"Yeah. Okay." He led her to that all-too-familiar doorway, then grabbed her arms and pulled her up against his body. "I miss you."

She missed him too, but she couldn't tell him that. "Austin, please, let me say this." Jane stepped back, but when she saw the pure terror in his eyes, her heart ached for him. "I'm sorry I got so angry with you last night. I didn't want us to end like that, so I want to explain how I felt."

He nodded, seeming to relax a little.

"You met someone else last night. That hurt, but not as much as you bailing out as soon as things got difficult."

"I'm not bailing out."

"Listen to me. Don't argue."

"I'm not arguing."

"Austin." Her eyes pierced him, and he backed up against the wall. "If you want to end this, that's fine." She choked back tears. Knowing she had nothing left to lose, she decided to gamble. "But do it for the right reason."

"I don't want to hurt you. What other reason do I need?"

"I don't believe that."

"You think I would hurt you?" He moved closer and reached out, but she backed away.

She couldn't let him touch her. That would drain what little defensive strength she had left. "No, I don't think that's the reason. You wanted someone else— "

He shook his head hard. "No, I don't want her."

" —and you're scared."

His eyes narrowed and he growled. "I am not scared."

She shot him a hard look, but he stood his ground. "You're afraid of trying to make this work so you're taking the easy way out." Saying it out loud brought back her anger, making her tone sharp.

"This is not easy! I told you that last night."

"Then be honest with me."

"I have always been honest with you."

"Then be honest with yourself." She advanced on him, and he froze.

"What the hell does that mean?"

"Tell me you don't want me anymore, and if *you* believe it, *I'll* believe it, and I'll let you go." She knew she was putting it all on the table, and waited for him to fold or call her bluff. But she wasn't bluffing, and he would not fold.

"I want you, Janie. Do you believe that?"

"Yes, I do. That's why I won't let you run away."

"I am not running— "

"Austin, you're not listening to me."

"You're not listening to *me*!"

"You said you don't want to hurt me. I understand that. You said you don't want that girl you met last night. That's great." She waited for him to argue again, but he stayed quiet. "Listen to me, now. You were tempted last night and it scared you. You didn't know what to do, so you did what you always do—you left."

"But you wouldn't let me."

"I don't want you to have any regrets. If it's over between us, it's over. No second chances."

"No, I don't want.... I don't know...." He ran his hands through his hair and turned away from her, bumping his head against the cold brick wall. When he turned to face her again, his desperate blue eyes were filled with honest fear. "Janie, I'm gonna be tempted again. I'm gonna hurt you and that's what scares me the most."

Ah-ha! There it is. That's the reason. The thought of hurting her scared him more than the thought of losing her. Jane summoned all the inner strength Jack and her mother claimed she possessed.

"I'm not afraid, Austin."

"Are you sure?"

She had to be. "Yes. We'll deal with your temptation as it happens."

"I don't know if I can—resist."

She understood; Austin Sinclair didn't know how to resist temptation—never had. "Everyone gets tempted. The important thing is you didn't give in."

"I kissed her."

"I know. You told me."

"Actually, she kissed me. I pushed her away."

"You can stop talking about it now."

"Sorry."

Jane closed the distance between them. She felt safe touching him now, and took his shaking hands. "Temptation by itself isn't bad. It's how you handle it that matters."

Austin looked into her eyes and squeezed her hands as if he needed strength from her. "Last night, I didn't know how to handle it."

"Yes you did. You told her no and then you came to see me, and if you weren't so bound and determined to run away from me—"

"Hey!"

"—we might've had a lot of fun last night."

"What are you talking about?"

"I hear makeup sex is pretty hot."

"I never thought...."

He looked so baffled she had to offer him some hope, some reason to believe they had a future. "I'm stronger than I look." *God, I hope so.* "I can handle it when you talk to another girl or smile at her. I'll be okay."

His eyes sparkled with unrelenting mischief. "Did you just give me permission to flirt with other women?"

Oh, how I missed those wicked blue eyes. "That's not exactly what I had in mind. I know how guilty you felt last night. Don't do that to yourself. You'll end up hurting us both."

"I don't like hurting you."

"It wasn't a whole lot of fun for me, either."

"I am *so* sorry."

"I know." She slid her arms around him and held him close, resting her head on his chest, soft and warm against her.

He wrapped his hands in her hair. "Am I forgiven?"

"For what?"

He leaned back and looked into her eyes. "For trying to take the easy way out."

"Yeah, don't do that again."

"I couldn't if I wanted to. You made it impossible."

"That'll teach you to bail out on me."

He touched her cheek. "You know I want you, so the only question is: do you want me?"

She couldn't resist the temptation to tease him. "Hmm... let me think about that."

Austin growled and kissed her, claiming her lips as his own. He forced his tongue into her mouth, taking what he wanted and giving her everything she needed. "Tell me you want me or I'll stop."

"I want you, Austin," she whispered on his lips.

"That's what I like to hear. Come to bed with me and let's make up."

"Ooo... I want to." She grabbed his wrist and turned his watch around. "But I have to get ready for my game."

"Damn it. All right, but tonight I won't let you run away from me." He pulled her close and nibbled her ear.

"I won't even try." She pushed away from him. "Are you coming?"

"I'm damn close."

She frowned at him over the top of her glasses.

"Oh, you're talking about the game." He winked.

Jane gave him one last kiss and ran off to the locker room. She didn't dare look back, afraid she would see something she wouldn't like. Had she done the right thing? Was fighting to stay with him worth the effort?

And he still wouldn't talk about the girl from high school. Did he still want her? Maybe he'd gotten past that, but he still feared anything resembling a serious relationship.

Oh God. Was Jane strong enough for both of them?

Chapter 16

Austin sat in the bleachers as Jane dribbled the soccer ball toward the goal. The damn goalie taunted her, but Jane just smiled. She faked a kick to the right and then—boom—pounded the ball left into the net as the goalie dove in the wrong direction.

"Goooooaallll!" the crowd cheered, Austin and Jack among them. The Bayfield Bears had just taken the lead.

"Jane took you back already?" Jack said to Austin. "How did you do that?"

"I didn't. She wouldn't let me break up with her." *Damn stubborn woman. How does she know me so well?*

Jack laughed. "Finally, a woman who won't let you run away."

"I was *not* running away."

Jack gave him a knowing look, but Austin ignored him, determined to follow Janie's every move.

"Okay, maybe I was. I'm surprised she didn't give up on me." He'd gone through a lot to get his Janie back, but she was worth it. Would it be this hard to keep her? He didn't mind. As long as she wanted him, he would do whatever was necessary. This would be the biggest challenge he ever faced, but he chose not to be afraid anymore.

"Maybe she thinks you're worth the trouble."

"Yeah, I guess so."

She knew he would be tempted again, and that he might try to take the easy way out again, but she'd listened when he told her he was afraid of hurting her. She still wanted to be with him, and even offered to help him. Was he really worth that much trouble?

"She said some things that made me think."

"Think about what?"

He hadn't meant to say that out loud. How could he explain it to Jack if he didn't understand it himself? "Lots of things." Could he tell her he feared getting hurt too?

"I like women who make me think."

Austin laughed. "Yeah, you would."

"Jane likes it when you hum."

"I do *not*—wait.... Janie likes it?"

Jack laughed, but he ignored him. Jane had just stolen the ball from the other team.

"Damn, she's good." Austin whistled and clapped.

"Scary too." Ryan plopped down next to them.

Austin snarled "What do you mean? You're the one who kicked her."

Ryan laughed. "Did she tell you how that happened?"

Austin shook his head. Jack stopped watching the game and listened.

"I was dribbling the ball down the field, getting ready to take a shot at the goal. Out of nowhere, Jane charges me. I couldn't stop my momentum. I kicked her—hard. She stole the ball and kept right on going like nothing happened."

Jack shook his head. "Scary is right."

Austin laughed. "That sounds like my Janie."

"The girl is a terror on the field." Ryan saw the way Austin was watching Jane's every move, cheering and shouting encouragement every chance he got. "You really like her."

Am I this obvious to everyone? "Yeah, I do."

"That's good. It's all about finding the right person." Ryan caught Austin's eye. "Treat her right."

"I will."

Finding the right person.... Someone who wouldn't put up with his BS. Someone who saw through his charm and called him on it. His mother let his father charm his way out of trouble for too long. She'd never held him accountable until the damage was beyond repair. Janie wouldn't do that. *Is Janie the right person for me?*

His parents thought they'd found the right person. His father had found the 'right person' more than once. No, that couldn't be right.

Jack had said he believed there was only one right person, and that once Austin found her, he wouldn't need—or want—to look for anyone else.

Ever since he'd met Janie, he'd forgotten all about looking for the next girl. Even the hot girl at McGinley's didn't interest him. He couldn't even remember her name. It didn't matter. Janie had to be the right girl for him. He couldn't imagine anyone else. He didn't want to.

He'd thought Natalie was the right person. Now he knew better, but at the time, it seemed so clear. Natalie had left him because she believed he never thought about the future. But he wasn't that guy anymore. How long would he let those memories drag him down? Could he finally let the past go and consider a future with Janie?

The final buzzer sounded as time expired. Janie and her team screamed and cheered. Bayfield had won 3-2. Jane ran off the field into Austin's arms.

He picked her up and spun her around, laughing with her. "You were amazing." He gave her a hard kiss right on the lips.

"I can't believe I made that shot." She leapt from Austin's arms and bear-hugged Jack.

"Their goalie couldn't believe it either." Jack patted her on the back.

"I feel like celebrating," she said.

"Where do you want to go, Janie?" Austin would go anywhere with her.

"Let's make it someplace quiet. I'm wiped out."

His mind whirled. She wouldn't be quiet for long.

"Oo—I know. Come over to my place. I made a cake last night, and I have a ton of it left."

"Mmm... what kind?" Both Austin and Jack wanted to know.

"Chocolate, caramel, toffee, whipped cream...."

"Oh, Janie, don't tease me." Austin pulled her close.

"Let me take a shower, and I'll meet you both back here."

"You're inviting me too?" Jack said.

"Sure. Why not? Be right back." Jane ran off to the gym.

"Is that okay with you, man?"

Austin actually didn't mind having Jack tag along. He liked hanging out with his two best friends. *Wow. What a weird thought.* "Sure. Why not? Whatever makes her happy."

Right then Austin knew that all he ever wanted was to make Janie happy. It didn't matter what his mother had said, what his father had done, or what Natalie had thought. Austin wanted love. No, he needed it; craved it. Could he take the chance?

He needed to talk to Jack about it, because his friend knew about love. Maybe they should invite Jack's girlfriend too, and then Austin could see how a couple in love were supposed to treat each other. "Where's Angie?"

Jack shrugged. "We're not seeing each other anymore."

"Sorry, man." *So much for that idea.*

"It's okay. I'm already interested in someone else."

"You sound like me." Austin laughed and corrected himself. "Like I used to."

"How do you like that?"

"I like it. Who is she?"

"No one you know."

"That narrows it down."

Jack laughed.

Austin watched Janie disappear into the gym, trying not to think about how close he'd come to losing her last night. He'd said no to Ava, doing that right at least, but he also remembered what he'd done wrong, what hurt Janie the most. He promised himself he'd never make that mistake again.

A stiff breeze blew across the open field and he shivered, remembering how cold he'd felt without Janie in his life. He didn't ever want to feel cold again.

***

Sara wasn't home when they got to the girls' apartment, and Austin breathed a silent sigh of relief.

"Make yourselves comfortable, guys." Jane ducked into the kitchen and brought them each a plate piled high with chocolate, caramel, and more chocolate, with whipped cream on top.

Austin grabbed a fork and dug in as she settled in next to him. "Wow."

Jack's plate was emptying fast. "This is so good. What's it called?" He made yummy noises and took another bite.

She smiled and blushed. "Um... it's called *Better than Sex Cake*."

"It is *not*," Austin protested. "It's great, but it's not better than sex."

She giggled, but didn't argue with him.

"Yes it is," Jack said.

"You need to get laid more often."

"Ya think?" Jack took another bite and moaned. "Austin told me you were a great cook, but I had no idea you could do this."

"Thank you." Jane smiled at Jack.

"I told you she cooked better than my mother, but you wouldn't believe me."

"I'll never doubt you again."

"Janie...." Austin put his empty plate on the coffee table, slid close to her, and nibbled her neck. "You are a goddess on the soccer field, in the kitchen...." He touched his lips to her ear. "...and in the bedroom. May I have some more?"

"You're talking about cake, right?"

Austin slid his hand under her shirt, teasing her bare skin. "For now."

"Since you asked so nicely...." She kissed him and got up.

"More for me too, please." Jack handed her his empty plate.

Jane gave them as much as they wanted, but she didn't eat anything. She alternately bit her lip and twirled her fingers in her hair, and Austin knew something was bothering her.

Was she still upset about last night? He thought they'd resolved that. What if she still had doubts about him? He felt an urgent need to talk to her, something he'd never cared to do before, but he didn't know how to start, so he praised her cake again.

"Janie, this is *almost* better than sex. You could be a chef."

"Definitely," Jack agreed.

"Thank you. I'm happy to hear you guys say that." This time she smiled when she bit her lip, looking at Austin, then Jack. Did she want to tell them something?

Austin put down his plate and squeezed her hand. "Talk to me, Janie."

Her eyes were still uncertain, but she gripped his hand tight. "Remember when I told you I haven't decided what I was doing with my major?"

"Yeah, I remember."

She took a deep breath. "I decided I'm going to culinary school after I graduate. I want to work in a restaurant for a while, and hopefully start one of my own someday."

"That's awesome," Jack said.

Austin nodded. "Do it. You'll be a great chef."

"Thank you. I'm a little nervous about it."

Was that all that was bugging her? Austin moved closer and kissed her, tugging at her lower lip with his teeth. "The only way you'll fail is if you don't try."

"I know." She snuggled against him, seeking comfort from his arms. "I needed to hear that."

"You'll be great," said Jack. "I'll be first in line when you open."

"No, I will," Austin argued.

"Don't think so," Jack shot back.

"I'll have my own personal chef." Austin grinned, thinking for the first time ever about having a future with a woman.

"Is that what you think?" Jane tried to scowl at him, but he didn't buy it.

"Uh-huh. You can serve me breakfast in bed, lunch in bed, dinner...." He kissed her, softly, sweetly, promising more.

"And what have you done to deserve all that?"

"I—" *Fell in love with you.*

Austin didn't deserve it—he didn't deserve a woman like her at all—but he loved her. His parents' messed up relationships, Natalie's rejection—all that pain and humiliation left him when he'd acknowledged he loved Janie. It scared him to death too, but Janie was smart and beautiful and had an inner strength he envied—and needed. He would probably end up hurting her, but until then he would love her as much as he possibly could.

He had to tell her. But he couldn't do it now, not with Jack there.

Then they heard the doorknob turn.

"Damn it, she has the worst timing," Austin grumbled.

Sara took two steps into the hallway and glared at Austin. Jack startled and waved. "Hey, Sara, you live here?"

"Yes." Sara's gaze moved from Austin to Jack, and her eyes softened a bit. "You didn't know that?"

"I knew Jane had a roommate named Sara." Psycho roommate, Jack had called her. "I didn't make the connection."

Sara fixed her eyes on Jane. "I thought you were going to tell me when he was here so I could avoid him."

"It was a spur of the moment thing," Jane said. "I didn't have time to tell you."

"Nice." Sara's eyes darkened. "I should've expected as much from you. He's a bad influence."

Jane's eyes turned shiny and wet. "Why are you being so mean?"

Austin moved closer to Jane. He'd faced defensive linemen three times his size every day without fear. He could take Sara's abuse, but he wouldn't let her go after Jane. "Leave Jane out of this. I'm the one you have a problem with."

"That's putting it mildly."

Austin stood up and stalked toward Sara, and she met him head on. "I'd like to know just what the hell your problem is."

Jack got to his feet and moved between them.

Sara snarled at Austin. "You don't remember."

He wished he could, but he had to admit he didn't. "Sorry. You'll have to enlighten me."

Sara ripped off her coat and threw it in the closet. "Second semester, freshman year. We dated."

He still didn't remember.

"It lasted longer than I expected it to—almost a month. I thought I'd changed you."

Sara... pretty, blonde, with a smile that lit up the room. Was she the same Sara facing him now?

"But no. Some ditzy cheerleader got your attention. You didn't even bother to dump me."

Jane sat on the couch, chewing her lower lip.

"Sara... I remember dark blonde hair, sexy blue eyes and big beautiful...." His eyes slid down her body to her breasts—

"Ahem."

--and then snapped back to her face. The blue eyes he remembered had once burned with lust, but now they burned holes right through him. "You didn't wear glasses back then."

"Brilliant, Einstein."

"No, I did break up with you." He didn't remember how exactly. "I always do."

"That's what you tell everyone, but I know it's not true."

Jane's face went white. "You cheated and you lied?"

"You cheated on me with—what's her name—Hayley. I'd like to say I was surprised...."

"Hayley! Now I remember."

"Great. You remember her." Sara's fingers curled and Jack grabbed her arm.

"Hayley was a hottie. I couldn't resist her."

Jack cringed. "Um, Austin, not good."

"I was young and stupid."

"You still are," Sara snapped.

"We both were. You thought you could change me, and I thought... I thought with my dick."

"You still do," Jack said, and Sara echoed his chuckle without any humor.

Austin ignored them. "I told you that maybe we should see other people, and I thought we were done."

Sara rolled her eyes. "I hate maybe. Do you know what 'maybe' means to a woman? It means there's hope. It means maybe you'll come back, maybe it's not over."

"Sara, I had no idea—"

"And then you forgot all about me! That really pissed me off. You've been with so many women, you can't even remember them all."

He couldn't deny it.

"If it helps, I didn't remember you'd dated Austin." Jack looked at Sara with an apology in his eyes. "I can't keep track of his women either."

"No, it doesn't help." Sara looked like she wanted to slap Jack, but snarled at Austin instead. "I got over you eventually, but seeing you with Jane brought it all back. I'm still over you, so don't go thinking I want you back. I just don't want you to hurt Jane the way you hurt me."

"I would never hurt Janie."

"I think you'd better tell her that, and you'd better hope she believes you. I wouldn't."

That pissed him off. "I don't care if you believe me or not! I broke up with you before I started seeing... what's her name. You got hung up on the word *maybe*. That's your problem, not mine."

"I don't care what your problem is. I gave up trying to figure that out a long time ago. Right now, you have bigger problems than me."

Austin turned to Jane, still sitting on the couch. Her swollen red lip stood out in sharp contrast against her pale skin. "Janie," he breathed.

Jane wouldn't look at him. She got up and took the dishes to the kitchen.

"I knew you would hurt her." Sara spun and walked out the door, leaving her coat, her keys and everything else behind.

"You take care of Jane," Jack said. "I'll go after Sara."

Austin started into the kitchen, but turned back. "What do I do? What do I say to her?"

"Don't say anything yet. Listen to her. Then you'll know what to do." Jack grabbed his coat and took off out the door.

Austin ducked through the kitchen door, running his hands through his hair. He watched Janie put away the cake, load the dishes in the dishwasher, wipe off the counter—doing everything but acknowledge him.

Listen. How hard can that be? It would be a lot easier if she would speak to him.

He couldn't stand the silence anymore. "Janie?"

Chapter 17

Oh God. He was lying. The knots in Jane's stomach tightened.

Austin had cheated on Sara, and he'd forgotten he even knew her.

Would the same thing happen with Jane? She thought she was going to be sick. Cheating, lying, one girl after another—all the rumors about Austin were true. Why hadn't she listened to Sara?

"Janie, please say something," Austin begged.

"I have one question for you."

Austin listened.

"How long will it take you to forget me?"

"Janie, I could never forget you."

"How do I know that's true?"

He didn't answer.

She finally turned and looked at him. "You were with Sara for a month, and you forgot all about her. We've only been together...." She counted on her fingers. "...a week and a half."

"Sara and I only had a few dates— "

"Did you sleep with her?"

Austin looked at her as if she were nuts. "Do you really have to ask?"

She threw him a disgusted look. "It doesn't even bother me that you slept with my roommate. What really makes me mad is that you didn't even remember what you'd done to her after you saw her again. Are you that heartless?"

***

Austin hadn't known his heart still worked until he'd met Jane. He hadn't known love was possible without hurt until she'd challenged him and made him change his way of thinking. Should he tell her that? Should he tell her she'd healed his heart? *Not yet.* She wasn't in the mood to listen to him, so he would take Jack's advice and listen to her.

"That's why Sara didn't want me to go out with you. She knew exactly what you were capable of. She knew you would leave me for the next pretty face you saw. It happened to her. It almost happened to me. How could I be so stupid to think that I would be the one to tame the heartbreaker? Me—plain Jane Elliot—finally got Austin Sinclair to settle down. Yeah, that could happen. God, I am such an idiot. After three years of sleeping with every girl on campus, you finally got around to me. Yeah, you'll settle for me, but not because you want to—because you're out of options."

"I'm not out of options!"

"Well, that's good to know."

"That's not what I meant. Damn it. I never settle for anything."

Jane was silent for a moment, considering what he'd said, and when she spoke, her voice was soft and calm. "I believe that."

He had no idea listening was so hard. He'd heard a lot of unpleasant things: he was a heartbreaker; he couldn't settle down; he wouldn't stay with Janie. No... she thought he might settle down, but she didn't think it would be with her. She didn't believe he would stay. That's what he heard. Was that what she was saying?

"Janie, do you believe that I want to be with you? That I'm here right now, facing a very angry, very scary woman because I choose to be here? I could be with anyone else right now." *God help me.* "I could've left with Jack, but I'm still here because I don't want to lose you. I have other options—damn it—and I sound like an idiot right now, because I've never done this before. You were right. I've always left at the first sign of trouble. I've never stayed and fought for what I wanted."

She didn't say anything; her turn to listen to him.

"I want you, in case you haven't figured that out yet, and I'm staying and fighting with you—*for* you."

She still didn't say anything, and he could see the doubt lingering in her eyes. Could he tell her he loved her? Would she believe him?

"I know," she said softly. "I know how hard it is for you to stay."

"Janie." He tried to pull her close, but she resisted. "I...." He couldn't find a way to say it. "I'm sorry for all of this. I never wanted to hurt you."

"I know." She came to him. "Just hold me for a while."

He wrapped her in his arms and held her tight. Her warm body warmed his empty soul and fearful heart.

***

Jane sighed and snuggled closer to Austin. She loved him, and couldn't deny it anymore. Why did she have to fall in love with him? He said he wanted her, but what did that mean? It felt so good to be in his arms and that was all that mattered. She would worry about feelings and meanings later.

"Where is your father?"

"You're thinking about my father?"

"I just want to be sure he isn't going to take you away from me tonight."

"Nothing can take me away from you. I'm all yours."

All hers... what a wonderful thought. Tonight she would believe it was true, and after that—

She refused to worry about after. Instead, she rode the sudden wave of happiness that swept over her. "Kiss me."

"I would but that lip looks like it hurts." Austin caressed her swollen lower lip with his thumb.

"I can take it."

"Think so?"

"Yes. Please?" She gave him her most tempting pout.

Austin held her face in his hands and kissed her, gently at first, being careful of her lip. When he knew he wasn't hurting her, he ran his hands more firmly through her hair, and pulled her head back, feasting on her lips like a man starved for affection.

She was equally starved for him. Neither one could get enough. They fell back against the kitchen counter, an urgent tangle of hands and tongues—tasting, touching, stroking. The buttons on her blouse gave no resistance, but she fumbled with his.

"Nope." Austin forced her hands back onto his shoulders. "I'm in charge this time."

She trembled.

"Do you like that?"

She bit her lip briefly before he kissed her again.

He pulled her blouse open, exposing her emerald green bra, pinching and kissing her hard nipples through the thin lace. "Ah, Janie." He sighed on her skin. "You are better than sex." He pushed her bra cups down so he could taste her naked breasts.

She arched back over the cabinets, giving him all he wanted, silently begging him to take more. His tongue circled her nipples, drawing them into his mouth. Her body heated in an instant, especially that aching spot between her legs.

Austin's hand slid down her bare stomach to the button on her jeans. He opened it and unzipped her, and cupped her face in his hands. There was still some fire flickering in her, left over from their fight. If he stoked it just right, and she expected he would, that passion would spark into an inferno they would never forget.

Jane's gasp turned into a moan. She knew he was good with his hands, but feeling him stroke her with his hard body was even better.

"Mmm... I know what my Janie likes."

Good God, does he ever! And he kept finding new things for her to like.

"You like it hard." He crushed her against the cabinet.

She gasped, taking the full weight of his hard body and wanting more.

"You like it hot." His heated words scorched her nipples.

She forgot how to breathe.

"And I'll bet you like it dirty." He spun her around, bent her forward and jammed his erection against her ass.

Oh, that's new. He closed his mouth on her neck, sending a trail of goose bumps down her body. She liked that already. Her knees buckled and he slid his arm around her waist, holding her tight against him. He slid his hand inside her jeans, seeking, stroking, and she spread her legs to give him more room. His fingers slid deeper.

"Don't stop," she moaned.

"Never." He yanked her jeans down to her knees, and her panties went with them. One hand caressed her nipples while the other slid between her legs, fingering her. "Come for me, Janie. Come hard."

The first wave crashed into her. She braced herself on the countertop, barely able to stand. The second knocked her back into Austin. The third would've sent her to her knees, but Austin held her up, impaled on his fingers.

"That's it, Janie. Ride it out."

She shuddered in his arms, catching her breath as his belt buckle clanked. Hearing him unzip was even hotter than seeing it. She leaned on the countertop, looking back over her shoulder. He had his cock in his hand, stroking himself as he prepared to enter her. She tried to spread her legs, but her jeans around her knees kept her firmly bound. His cock slid between her tightly squeezed thighs, dragging against her hot, wet flesh as he leaned over her again.

***

She was so hot and tight he could barely think straight. Austin turned her face and kissed her, pretending to search for her entrance with his cock.

"There are times for slow and gentle," he whispered hot into her ear. "This is not one of those times." He grabbed her hips and slammed it home.

Jane cried out, reaching up to grab the cabinets and thrust back against him. Her entire body shook, and she let out a little squeal, her thighs trembling and her skin getting hot. She arched and let out a wail that would have frightened the neighbors. Austin held her while she rode it out, giving her soft kisses on her back and shoulders.

Oh God, I'm going to come. He couldn't stop it; he didn't want to stop it. He'd never known a girl who could get him off so quickly and leave him wanting more. *Damn, it feels so good.*

He closed his eyes and let the explosion rip through his entire body, leaving him sweaty and shaking. He rested on Jane's back, feeling her still throbbing around him. A happy little smile curled his lips as he felt that familiar tingle. He was far from finished.

Give him a few minutes and he would take her all over again. He just had to figure out what to do with her in the meantime.

"Let's see how many times I can make you come." He lifted her onto the counter, spreading her legs as he sank to his knees. He freed her from her jeans and threw them on the floor.

***

"Oh," Jane gasped, leaning back on her hands.

She felt exposed in that position, especially since she was naked and he was still dressed. Exposed, vulnerable, and... dirty. Yeah, she liked that. Having Austin's mouth between her legs made her feel—oh God—so naughty. Listening to him moan and make yummy noises while he licked her nearly made her giggle. He was enjoying it as much as she was.

Oh, that feels so.... Would she ever get enough? *Oh—yes—more, more, more!*

She shifted her weight and lifted one hand to touch her nipple. Yes, that's what she needed. Austin slid a couple of fingers inside her. Yes, she needed that too.

"Please," she said.

She knew what she was begging for this time, and that he could give it to her. She just had to be patient and wait for him to find that perfect spo—

Oh yes! right there! Her hips lifted right off the counter.

"There's number one." Austin kissed the inside of her thighs while he waited for her to come back down.

"I think that was number three."

He laughed and touched her with his tongue. She squirmed and gasped, ready for more, and ran a fingertip across her nipple.

"Help me out," he said, taking her hand and guiding it between her legs, playing inside her with his tongue while she made circles with her fingers.

Jane wasn't uncomfortable touching herself, but she'd never imagined doing it with someone else. This definitely felt dirty, especially with Austin looking at her. She closed her eyes so she couldn't see him watching. When she did it herself, it could take a while, but this wasn't going to take long at all.

Austin traded places with her, twisting his finger with hers and pushing them inside her while he licked her pulsing nub. "I want you to feel what I feel when you come."

If he kept saying things like that, she was going to die coming. At the moment, she didn't care. She felt her body tighten around their fingers, clenching and releasing. She felt moisture and heat—oh so much heat. *Is this what he feels when he's inside me? Tight, wet, hot—oh God—tighter and hotter still.*

Jane's body curled and she lost her balance, but Austin caught her, both of them breathing hard. "Oh, Austin, how can you stand it?"

"Are you kidding?" He looked around the kitchen and spotted a straight-backed chair. "I can't get enough of you." Bracing the chair against the cabinets, he sat down and pulled her onto his lap.

She kissed him hard while he shifted under her, entering her with a sharp upward thrust that made her gasp. "Slow and gentle?" she asked, with a wicked sparkle in her eyes.

"Oh hell no!"

He wrapped his arms around her waist and slammed hard. Jane rode him, bracing her hands against the countertop when the chair nearly tipped over. It scooted across the floor with every thrust. They laughed and kissed.

"We're going to end up on the floor." Jane giggled on his lips.

"No problem," Austin grunted. "I'll fuck you on the floor too."

A wild thrill shot through her body at the thought. "You are pure evil."

"Ha! There's nothing pure about me."

He snarled and bit down on her neck just above her shoulder, sending a roller coaster ride of tingles and chills through her, curling her fingers and her toes. He held her tight, taking her with him when their ride rocketed out of control.

Jane's world spun. The chair tipped. She was falling, flying, and then landing safe in Austin's arms, resting her cheek on his strong shoulders.

She lifted her head, surprised they were still upright in the chair. "Had enough yet?"

"Nope." He laughed and kissed her. "But we need to move to your bed. This chair is not comfortable."

"I'm surprised we didn't flip it over."

"I've done that. Nearly busted my head open. One time I...."

She laughed. "At least you learn from your mistakes."

He kissed her and slipped his hand between her legs, as if trying to distract her.

"Mmm... Austin, you are *such* a bad boy."

"But you like me. You told me so."

"Shut up and go to my room."

"Just show me the way."

"And take your clothes off. Why am I the only one naked?"

"Cuz that's the way I like it." He spanked her bare ass and ran down the hall.

Chapter 18

It didn't take her long to get him naked, but then, Austin couldn't think of a single reason to keep his clothes on. There was nothing better than feeling Janie's bare skin on his. Yep, he could definitely get used to that, and for once, the thought of getting used to a girl didn't bore him. In fact, it excited him.

For the first time in his life, he didn't want to send a girl home as soon as he'd finished with her. He wanted to keep her close and learn more about her. He wanted to know what she liked and dreamed about and cared about. He already knew some of those things, but he wanted to know more. He wanted to know her—his Janie.

"I like my bed better with you in it." She sighed and snuggled close.

Austin put his arm around her and kissed the top of her head. "It doesn't matter whose bed we're in. As long as I'm with you, I'm happy." *Holy shit. I* am *humming.*

She stroked his shoulder with her fingertips. "You never told me about dinner with your dad. How did that go?"

He groaned. "Do you really wanna know?" The humming stopped.

She rolled onto his chest and locked eyes with his. "Yes, I do."

He put his arms around her and massaged her back. He couldn't remember when anyone else cared to listen. Even Jack didn't want to hear about it anymore. "The bad news is he doesn't like you."

"I already knew that. And the good news?"

"He couldn't make the waitress cry."

She cringed. "Maybe you're being too hard on him."

"I'm not, trust me. You only had to spend a few minutes with him. I've been putting up with his BS all my life."

"Why doesn't he like me?" She made lazy circles on his skin.

"He didn't give me a good reason. He said you weren't good enough for me, he didn't like your glasses...."

"He doesn't like my glasses?"

"I love them—sexy librarian—mmm." She'd taken off her glasses at some point during their romp in the kitchen, but he couldn't remember when. "He thought the bruise on your knee was hideous."

"Well, we have that in common. What did he say when you told him how well you patched me up?"

He hesitated. "I didn't tell him."

"Why not?"

Damn, she's persistent. "I haven't told him about my future plans."

"So he still thinks you're going to play in the NFL?"

"Most likely, since I haven't told him otherwise."

"Austin...."

"I don't know how to tell him."

"'Dad, I'm going to be a doctor, not a football player'."

"Yeah, you'd think it would be that easy, but...."

"But?"

What could he tell her that didn't sound like an excuse? All his reasons were excuses, but up until now, he'd thought they were good ones. "He won't listen to me. He never does. All through dinner, I tried to tell him how great you are and how much I care about you, but he still thinks your name is Jean."

Janie was drawing circles over his heart with her finger, but she stopped and raised her head.

"How do I get it through his thick skull?"

He was surprised to see a goofy smile playing across her face.

"Janie?"

"Huh? Oh sorry. I just hate being called Jean."

"What do I do?"

He'd never asked for help before, but this was the second time tonight. Did she think he was weak? Was that why she wasn't answering him?

She touched his worried face. "You have to make him listen."

"How?" He knew how to make a woman do anything he wanted, even one as stubborn as Jane, but had no idea how to get his father to pay attention to him just once.

"The first time I told my mother I wanted to go away to school, she blew me off, so when I got accepted here, I made her sit down, took away anything that might distract her, and wouldn't let her argue with me until I was done talking."

"Did she argue?"

"For days, but at least I knew she'd heard me, even though she didn't like it."

"How did you win?"

"I stopped arguing with her. She couldn't fight with me if I didn't fight back. I just let her vent and eventually she ran out of complaints. Then she started listening to me."

"She doesn't complain anymore?"

"Every chance she gets, but it's the same old, same old. It's easier to ignore her when she's a thousand miles away."

"I wish my dad was a thousand miles away. I should've gone to a different school."

"I'm glad you didn't." She laid her head on his chest.

"I am too." He was learning so much from her. If he somehow managed not to hurt her; if he was able to keep her in his life and make her happy; he could only imagine how happy he would be, loving her. "It won't be like the last time."

"Huh?"

"I fell for this girl in high school. I loved her, but she dumped me because I had no plan for the future."

"Who plans their future in high school? Most people don't know what they want to do with their lives until they finish college. Some *never* figure it out."

"Good point."

He'd changed his major a couple times, and Jack didn't declare his until last year, but he still didn't know what kind of career he was looking for. Well hell, if Jack didn't know what he wanted as a senior in college, then Austin couldn't be blamed for not knowing when he was a senior in high school.

"That was *her* excuse, wasn't it?"

"Probably. Maybe she was embarrassed to admit the real reason."

He shrugged. "Doesn't matter. The only thing that matters to me is having you in my arms."

He ran his hands through her silky hair, and pulled her up for a kiss, loving the feel of her body sliding across his chest. He rolled on top of her, parting her thighs with his knees, sinking into her so deep he thought he would lose himself in her. That was what he wanted more than anything else—all Janie, all the time.

There could never be anything better.

***

Something woke Jane up. It was the middle of the night, but the bedside lamp was still on. She wanted to turn it off, but couldn't reach, and Austin was using her as his pillow. His head nestled between her breasts and a happy smile occupied his face.

There was no way she was going to disturb him. She'd keep him there forever if she could.

She sighed and tried to go back to sleep. Those annoying doubts were sneaking up on her again. *So he loved a girl once. And she broke his heart. That's a good reason for swearing off relationships.*

Even though she'd been dying to know about that girl, she'd still bristled when Austin admitted he'd loved her. Could he love Jane as much as he'd loved that girl?

The last time they'd made love, it felt like making love—slow and gentle, passionate and intense, their bodies so close she couldn't tell where he ended and she began. Their fingers had remained laced together. Kissing soft and sweet. Kissing hard and deep.

He'd whispered and moaned the most wonderful words to her... but not the words she needed to hear.

Austin sighed in his sleep and brushed his lips on her skin.

She ran her fingers through his soft hair, careful not to wake him. Before he'd fallen asleep, he'd told her she'd worn him out. He called her his Janie, then yawned and closed his eyes. She didn't need to ask him to stay. She knew he wouldn't leave.

Maybe that was enough. Maybe those three words were overrated. Maybe someday Austin would figure out how to say them. Maybe.... *Ugh!*

She definitely knew why Sara hated the word maybe.

***

The first thing Austin saw when he woke up was Janie's naked breast. He leaned over and kissed it, liking the way she stirred beneath him. Then he saw the clock. *Damn it, I'm gonna be late.* He pressed soft kisses and tiny nips on Janie's skin until she woke up.

"Mornin', beautiful."

"Already?"

"Yup."

She groaned and turned over. He'd worn her out last night, but she'd kept up with him, and now that he thought about it, she'd done the same to him. He'd slept so well cuddled up with her as his pillow. He needed to do that more often—and forever.

He groaned. He had to figure out how to tell her that. Why was it so hard? *I love you, Janie.* The words echoed in his head, but he couldn't get them past his lips.

Yes, he could. They were just words—words that meant absolutely everything to him. "I love you, Janie," he whispered.

But she was asleep.

He really would be late if he didn't get up now. He ran his hands over her body until she opened her eyes.

"What are you doing?" she moaned.

"Taking advantage of you."

"Mmm... please continue."

"I'd like to, but I have to go. Coach wants us at warm-ups early today."

"Oh yeah." She sat up, holding the sheets in front of her. "Today is the game against State."

"Yup." He yanked the sheets down to her hips.

"Hey!" She tried to pull them back up.

"Now you get shy?" He laughed and kissed her. "What did you do with my clothes?" He got up and searched the room.

"I'm not telling." She let the sheets drop, and plopped back against the pillows. She lay there naked, hair in knots, pushing the sheets further and further down.

What am I supposed to be doing? "And you call me evil."

"You are." She stuck her tongue out at him.

Austin dropped his pants on the floor and crawled on top of her. "Just wait till tonight. I'll show you what happens to girls who tease."

"Is that a promise?" Her hands slid down his stomach.

"Oh hell yes." He kissed her, sliding his fingers inside her, stroking her with his thumb until she started to squirm.

"Oh please...."

With a laugh that proved he really was the evil one, Austin stood up and threw the covers over her. "Stop distracting me, woman."

She sat up sputtering and pulled the blankets off her head. "That was just mean."

"Yeah, but you liked it." He pulled his jeans on while she tempted him, touching her body where he should have been touching her. Lunging for the bed, Austin grabbed the blanket and pulled it up to her neck. "Are you coming to the game?"

"Yes, I am. I'll look for you. What position do you play again? Left bench?"

"Ha ha. I'm the guy with the big number seven on my back throwing touchdowns."

"Number seven. Got it." She puckered her lips for a kiss.

"You are just too cute." He kissed her gently. "I gotta go. Bye." He stopped short at her bedroom door. "I mean...."

"I know. Go away, already."

He blew her a kiss and nearly ran over Sara in the kitchen.

"Good morning, Austin." Sara even managed a tired smile.

"Good morning."

"Do you want some coffee?"

Is it poisoned? "Um... no thanks. I need to get to practice."

"Jack told me you're playing State today. Good luck."

"Thanks." He wanted to run for the door, but if she was being nice to him, he had to make an effort back. "How are you?"

She gave him a weak smile. "Better."

"Good." He gave her a nod. "I gotta go, but I'll probably see you later... with Jane... and Jack."

"Probably."

He put his hand on the doorknob, but before he opened it, he stopped and looked at Sara. "I know you want to protect Janie. You don't want to see her hurt. I don't either. We have that in common."

"Yes we do." Sara nodded.

"Good." At least they agreed on something. "Come to the game, if you don't have other plans, and bring my girl with you." He nearly bounced off the wall as he darted out the door.

Damn it, I'm humming again.

***

"Morning, Sara." Jane wandered into the kitchen, following the scent of coffee. "How are you?"

"I'm okay."

Jane brought her coffee out to the living room and sat down in the overstuffed chair, yawning.

"You look like hell," Sara said. "Austin looked happy. Did you guys kiss and make up?"

Oh, yeah. "Uh-huh."

"That's good."

"Really?"

"Good for *you*. I don't care about Austin," Sara grumbled.

Well, that's better than hating him. "Where did you go last night? Did Jack find you?"

"He caught up with me in the park. We talked for a long time."

"That's good." Jane had made up with Austin, and it looked like her roommate and boyfriend weren't at each other's throats this morning, but she knew things still weren't right between Sara and her. "I'm sorry I brought Austin over without telling you first."

"Thank you. I appreciate that."

"But you need to understand that Austin is part of my life now, and I...."

Sara looked at her coffee.

"I don't want him to come between us." Jane moved over to the couch and touched Sara's knee with her shaking hand. "I miss you."

"I miss you, too." Her voice cracked.

"Do you think you can find a way to forgive Austin?"

Sara let out a heavy sigh and drank deep from her coffee cup. "I might... when I know he won't do the same thing to you."

"Do you think he will?" Even after everything they'd gone through last night, Jane's heart panicked at the thought that Austin might hurt her too.

Sara sighed. "Jack told me a lot of things about Austin last night."

"Really? He wouldn't tell me anything about Austin." *Nothing important anyway.*

"He told me Austin has grown up a lot since he met you, that he figured out there's more to a relationship than getting laid."

"He told me he was in love with a girl in high school. I think that's the only relationship he's ever had."

"He never said anything to me about her." Sara finished her coffee. "But apparently Austin still has a lot to learn."

"Tell me about it." She sighed.

"But he thinks Austin's devoted to you."

Hope filled her heart. "Jack said that?"

"How did he put it?" Sara laughed. "Austin's bat-shit crazy over you."

Jane laughed with her. "I believe that."

"I believe it too, and now that I'm reasonably sure Austin isn't the selfish pig he used to be, I think I can tolerate having him around."

Well, that was progress, but was it enough to heal the rift between her and Sara? "Can you forgive me?"

"Oh sweetie." Tears filled Sara's eyes and she grabbed Jane in a sudden hug. "You didn't do anything wrong."

"I didn't listen to you." Jane sobbed, hugging her back. "You told me he was a heartbreaker, but I fell in love with him anyway."

"Yes, he is, but I think he has his hands full with you."

Jane sat back and wiped tears from her eyes. "That's what he says."

"I almost feel sorry for him!"

"Yeah, poor guy." Jane giggled. "He doesn't know what hit him."

They laughed and cried and laughed some more. Finally, Jane got up and wiped her face, done with her tears.

"I'm starving. Do you want me to make breakfast?"

"Sounds good. I'm hungry too."

She bounced off to the kitchen. Eggs, bacon, ham, cheese.... "Hey, Sara, do you want to go to the game with me?"

"Sure, why not?"

"Cool. I can't wait." She skipped back to the kitchen, but stopped in mid-hop, horrified. "Oh my God, am I bouncing?"

"Yes, you are."

"Argh. I really didn't want that to happen."

But it *had* happened, and there was nothing she could do about it.

***

Austin met Jack on the sidelines. "Makeup sex—wow. Best night of my life." But it was more than hot sex; it was being with Janie that had made it the best.

Jack laughed. "You've never had makeup sex before?"

"I've never made up with anyone before."

"Hopeless."

"I saw Sara this morning. She was... pleasant. What did you do to her?"

A hint of a smile touched Jack's lips. "That's my little secret."

"You dog."

Jack changed the subject. "Pay up. I saw your dad in the stands."

"Damn it."

Jack scanned the bleachers for Sara and Jane. "Uh-oh."

"What?"

"Your dad has a cute young blonde with him."

Austin followed Jack's gaze. "A new trophy wife? I would've heard about that."

Charles Sinclair Jr. spotted them, nudged the pretty blonde, and pointed to Austin. She beamed and waved at him, blowing him a kiss.

"I think this one's meant to be *your* trophy."

"You have *got* to be kidding me. I hope Janie didn't see that." Austin found Jane and Sara sitting dangerously close to his dad and the blonde.

"Don't worry. Sara will back you up."

Austin wrenched his eyes from the frightening scene in the bleachers and looked at Jack. "Seriously? How did you manage that?"

"I'm very persuasive."

Austin laughed. "I'm glad you finally started listening to me for a change." He waved to Janie, then forced himself to focus on the game.

The opening minutes started with typical Austin Sinclair style—throwing a forty-six-yard touchdown pass to Greg on the very first play.

"Show off," Jack said.

Austin laughed. "The next one's yours."

State scored on their first possession, but Austin led the Bears' offense right back down the field to the three yard line, where Jack plowed through State's formidable defense to put his team ahead. The lead changed with every possession, and at halftime, the score was tied.

***

"This is so nerve-wracking," Jane said.

Sara's eyes were glued to the field. She was busy trying not to bite her fingernails. "I never understood why everyone at this school worshipped Austin, but he's actually a pretty good quarterback."

"Pretty good?"

"Oh, all right, he's awesome," Sara admitted. "But don't tell him I said that. It'll go to his head."

"Too late. He already thinks he's God's gift to football... and women."

"Hold it together, Austin!" Charles stood and clapped as the Bears ran back on the field.

"That's Austin's father." Jane nodded toward him, three rows down and five seats to their right.

"Oh yeah. I can see where Austin gets his good looks."

"He doesn't have half Austin's charm. He's a jerk." Jane shuddered. "Austin's no saint, but this guy...."

"Jack told me about him."

"What else did he tell you?"

Whatever Sara might have said was drowned out by the erupting crowd. The Bears had just kicked off to start the second half.

***

State got the ball and the lead first. Austin threw a beautiful touchdown pass on the next drive, but a holding penalty called it back, and they had to settle for a field goal.

Austin got hit hard and often during the third quarter, but he picked himself up every time, walking off the pain.

"How's that knee?" Jack asked.

"Hurts like hell." Austin gritted his teeth. "Don't tell Coach."

"Give me the ball. I'll take the hits for a while."

Austin knew Jack could take the punishment. "Sounds good to me."

Jack ran most of the plays during the fourth quarter, taking time off the clock. They held on to a slim lead, but in the final seconds, State scored another touchdown.

The Bears returned the kickoff past midfield, but now only four seconds remained. Austin stared at the scoreboard—five points behind and twelve yards to go. There was only enough time for one more play, and Austin knew what it had to be. He signaled Coach and the older man nodded.

Austin joined the team in the huddle. "A field goal won't cut it. We need a touchdown. I want everyone who can catch to get in the end zone. I'll throw to anyone who's open."

Austin took the snap and dropped back, scanning the end zone for an open man. Jack... no. Aaron... no. Donald... no. Greg... yes! Austin threw the ball with perfect accuracy but too much force. It bounced out of Greg's hands and hit the ground as time ran out.

Austin sank to his knees and pulled off his helmet, hanging his head.

The crowd groaned, and somewhere out of the corner of his eye, Austin saw his father shake his head.

Jack trotted down the field and put his hands on Austin's shoulders. "You did your best. We can't ask for anything more." Jack helped him up as the rest of the team surrounded them.

"I should've had that one, man." Greg shook his head. "I'm sorry."

"No," Austin said. "I knew I'd thrown it too hard as soon as it left my hand. You're lucky I didn't take your head off."

They walked to the sidelines where their fans stood cheering and clapping. All their fans except Austin's father.

Jane ran to Austin and threw her arms around him. "You were amazing. I'm sorry it ended like that."

He pulled her close. Holding her had never felt so good, and somehow having her there made losing easier to bear. "I'm so glad you're here."

"I'll always be here."

"Janie, I— "

"What the *hell* did you think you were doing?"

Chapter 19

Austin's smile froze when he saw the look on his father's face.

"Did you really think you could make that throw?"

"Yes, I did." Austin squared his shoulders and stepped in front of his father.

Jack stood right beside him, solid as a rock. "Anyone else would've thrown an interception."

"I've seen him make tougher throws than that." Sara moved beside Jack.

"We all have." Jane looked Charles in the eye. "And that includes you."

"At least your cheerleaders believe in you," Charles sneered. "But they won't impress the sports agents. You need to do that on your own."

Austin rolled his eyes. "We're not having this conversation again."

"Yes, we are. You don't seem to be getting it."

"*I'm* not getting it?"

"This is your senior year. This is your last chance to enter the draft."

Austin's jaw clenched, but he didn't say a word.

Jane moved closer and put her arm around his waist. Jack crossed his arms over his chest and glared at Charles. Sara's expression was just short of pity.

It was long past time to tell his father everything. Austin knew his father wasn't in the mood to listen, but he would tell him anyway. Encouraged by the support of his friends, Austin decided he was done letting Charles Sinclair Jr. dictate his future.

"Dad, there's something you need to know."

"Damn it, Austin, this is your career we're talking about." Charles started pacing in front of the four friends.

"No, it's not."

"Your next game has to be flawless."

"No, it doesn't." Since Austin had chosen his own path, he'd started playing football for the fun of it, and was enjoying it a lot more.

"I've got some connections. I'll make a few calls and get someone with influence to come to your next game." Charles pulled out his cell phone.

"No, you won't."

"It's no problem. All I need to do is—"

"Dad, you need to shut up and listen to me for once in your life!"

Charles stopped short, clicked his phone off and stared at Austin. "What?"

"Listen to me." He looked his father in the eyes, as if that would open his ears. "I'm not going to play in the NFL."

"That's not funny." Charles brushed him off and resumed dialing.

"I'm not joking. I'm not entering the draft." Austin held his ground, waiting for his father to turn back.

"You still have time." Charles put the phone to his ear. "Hey, Edward, how are you? Listen, you need to see my son play—"

"Dad! Listen to what I have to say, and don't say another word until I'm finished." Austin grabbed his phone and tossed it to Jack. "Got it?"

"What the hell?" Charles crossed his arms over his chest and stared his son down.

Austin swallowed hard. "I never fully recovered from that knee injury freshman year. I talked to a few coaches and agents and they told me I might get drafted, but I'd never play as a starter, and I probably wouldn't play more than a couple of years. I talked to Mom about it and—"

"Your mother knows?"

"Let me finish. Mom encouraged me to find another career. She helped me find out what my other interests and talents were."

"She never told me."

"She left that up to me. I decided I wanted to pursue sports medicine. I want to help other athletes like me."

"Sports medicine?"

"Yes." Austin fought the temptation to defend his choice, but he decided he didn't have to explain anything more.

"So you'll be what—a trainer?" Charles spat the word.

"While I'm in med school, and then I plan to be a team doctor."

"Why not a coach? Coaches get Super Bowl rings."

Austin shook his head. "This is what I want to do. It's my choice."

That finally shut Charles up, but not for long. "And you make such great choices. Just look at Jean here and compare her to Brittany." He gestured to the smiling blonde sitting all alone in the bleachers.

Austin shook his head. Apparently, the term girlfriend meant nothing to his dad.

He looked at Brittany. The girl was beautiful, with a beaming smile and hair the color of the sun, and she wasn't afraid of showing off her mounds of cleavage whenever he looked her way. She was exactly his type.

He noticed that Jane bit her lip when he took his arm away and put his hands on his hips. He stared at the pretty blonde practically offering herself to him. Austin licked his lips, and Jane looked like she was going to be sick.

Charles rambled on. "She's pretty, she's perky, and when you get bored with her, she's easily replaced."

Jane and Sara gasped. Even Jack raised an eyebrow.

Austin looked at Brittany one last time and shook his head, then took his girlfriend's hand and faced his father. "You know, Dad, I used to think I was just like you—love 'em and leave 'em. No girl could hold on to me. I had a new girl every weekend. Hell, I could have a new girl every day of the week if I wanted to. I was the campus stud, the campus heartbreaker. I enjoyed it, was proud of it, even. But I was so busy using your pathetic failed relationships as an excuse for my pathetic behavior, that I didn't know I was hurting anyone."

Then it hit him. He had hurt women. He had made them cry. He'd done everything his mother had warned him not to.

He turned to Sara and took a deep breath. "Sara, I am so sorry I hurt you. You deserved better."

She smiled, blinking back a couple of tears. "Thank you, Austin."

"Oh please." Charles rolled his eyes.

"The funny thing is, Dad, that I just figured out I don't have to be like you. I don't *want* to be like you. I can be happy with one woman because I choose to be."

"You're young, Son. You have no idea what real life is like."

"You weren't around when I was in high school, so you don't know what I've been through. Life was a bitch back then, but I got through it without you."

"Is that what you want? Do you want me to leave you alone?"

"No, Dad, I just want you to back off a little—okay, a lot—and if I'm gonna make a mistake, let me make it."

Charles cast a meaningful look at Jane.

"Jane is not a mistake. I love her and I'm not going to let her go." Austin pulled her close.

She buried her face in his chest, blinking back tears and hiding her smile from his father. Jack and Sara didn't bother to hide theirs.

Charles frowned. "So this is what you want—sports medicine, Jean–"

"Jane!" four people shouted.

Charles cleared his throat. "Jane." He scanned her up and down, sizing her up. Then he sighed. "All right then, *Jane*, Take care of my son."

"I will."

"Austin, take care of yourself. I'll be at your next game... if you want me to."

"I always want you at my games."

"That's good to know. I'm sorry I've missed some." Charles extended his hand.

"I know." Austin shook his father's hand. "I'll see you next weekend."

"Good. Don't let Jack do all the work next time. I don't think he can take it."

Charles dismissed them with a nod, and collected his phone and Brittany.

"I don't know about the rest of you," Jack said, "but that guy could drive me to drink."

Austin grunted. "Sounds good to me."

"Do you think he'll ever change?" asked Sara.

Jack shook his head and mouthed the word no.

"Probably not," Austin admitted, watching his father walk away. "But I did, so maybe he can too."

"I don't think you changed," said Jack. "I think you've been a good guy all along."

"No, don't say that." Austin faked a groan.

"You just needed the right person to help you figure that out."

"Hmm... I wonder who that could be." Austin squeezed Janie.

She kissed him. "I have no idea. I certainly haven't figured you out."

"Good. I don't want you to get bored with me."

"Never."

"I love you. You heard that part, right?"

Jane looked at him, her eyes shining like brilliant green emeralds. "I did. I love you too."

It was amazing how three simple words erased all his pain and fear. "You did it, Janie. You changed my mind. You healed my heart." He pulled her close. "You were right."

She cuddled against his chest, listening to his heart. "No. You changed my mind. Love doesn't just work out. It takes work. We're both right."

Austin picked her up and spun her around until they were both dizzy. They were still laughing when he kissed her, claiming her lips and her heart as his own. "Now *this* is better than sex."

"I'm not sure I believe that," Jane teased him, seeking another kiss.

"Oh yeah? I love you, Jane." Kiss. "Marie." Kiss. "Elliot." Austin felt that kiss all the way to his heart.

"Enough, already." Sara smacked Austin upside the head. "Let's get something to eat. I'm starving."

"Lead the way."

Austin put his arms around the girls' shoulders while they joined hands behind his back. Jack slid his arm around Sara's waist, linking the four friends together. Controlling parents, painful pasts, and nagging doubts were all forgotten, and the only things that really mattered—friendship and love—stayed with them.

"You lost our bet, so you're buying," Jack told Austin.

"Fair enough. Where do you want to go?"

"McGinley's!"

"You heard the ladies," Jack grinned.

"Works for me." Austin pulled Jane closer. "As long as I can get my hands on your fries again."

Jane's wicked green eyes flashed all sorts of naughty promises. "Oh, I've got much better things you can get your hands on."

While Jack laughed, Sara rolled her eyes. "I knew he was a bad influence on her."

Austin ignored them. "Oh, baby, you know what I like." Then he realized what he'd said and put his lips to her ear. "Sorry, I wasn't calling you baby."

"I don't mind so much."

"Oh yeah?" Austin tested her. "Sweetheart?"

"That's okay, too."

"How 'bout if I call you my kick-ass soccer goddess?"

Jane laughed. "I like that one."

"Just remember she can kick your ass." Sara winked at him.

"I'll never forget." Austin stepped back, taking Janie with him for a full-body-contact kiss. "Tell me you want me."

She melted in his arms. "I want you."

He held her face in his hands and looked into her eyes, giving her that happy smile she loved so much. "Tell me you love me."

"I love you, Austin Sinclair." She kissed him. "Always."

"That's what I like to hear."

Austin turned to the others. "Hey, Sara, your roommate's prettier than mine. Wanna trade?"

Epilogue

"Charlotte! Don't think I can't see what you're doing," Jane warned. "Those cookies are not for you."

Big innocent blue eyes peeked over the table. "Please, Mommy?"

"No. Those are for my customers."

The pretty three-year-old stomped her little foot, ran to her father, and climbed into his arms. "If you let me have a cookie, I'll give you a kiss." She gave him her sweetest pout.

"Oh, she's got that down," Austin groaned.

Jack laughed. "She knows exactly how to play you."

"I'll tell you what, Sweetie. If you get me one too, I'll tell your mother it was my idea."

"Okay."

"And I'll give you a kiss no matter what." Austin hugged her and planted a big smooch on his daughter's cheek. "I love you."

She threw her arms around his neck and scurried off across the dining room.

"I love being Daddy." Austin smiled at the sneaky little girl with her mother's silky brown hair and her father's naughty blue eyes.

"Your dad was right," Jack said.

"About what?"

"It does take more than one girl to make you happy."

Austin laughed, trying not to give his daughter's mission away by watching too closely. Charlotte hid behind the table, waited until her mother and Aunt Sara weren't looking, and then snatched two cookies.

"Charlotte Jane!" Mommy saw her run back to Daddy with her prize. "Austin, you're supposed to be watching her."

"I *am* watching her. I'm watching her steal your cookies." He took a bite of a cookie and winked at his wife.

Sara laughed. "You have a mini-Austin on your hands."

Jane clapped her hand over her mouth so the two culprits wouldn't see her laughing. "I know. They're so scary."

***

Jane checked the dining room to make sure everything was ready. Finally, after months of preparation, she could say it looked good. Sara followed her back to the kitchen, so Jane could give her staff a few last-minute instructions.

When she finally felt prepared, she breathed a shaky sigh. "I could use a glass of wine. Do you want one, Sara?"

"Yes, please."

Jane's hands trembled as she poured the wine.

"Nervous?"

"What if no one shows up? Did I do all this for nothing?"

"No need to worry about that." Austin strode into the kitchen, carrying his little cookie thief. "Your first patrons just arrived."

"Really?" Jane peeked out the kitchen door and watched her hostess seat their guests. More people were waiting behind them.

"Congratulations, Janie." Austin pulled her close and kissed her. "You're a chef in your own restaurant. I knew you could do it."

"Yay, Mommy!"

"To Chef Jane!" Sara raised her glass.

"What are you doing with that?" Jack snatched the still-full glass from his wife's hand. "You can't have wine."

Sara gasped. "Oh, sorry, I forgot."

Jane pulled away from Austin. "Why can't you...?" But when she saw Sara's eyes light up, she didn't need to finish her question. "You're pregnant!"

Sara nodded and hugged her friend.

"It's about time you knocked her up." Austin punched Jack's arm.

"Hey, it's not for lack of trying."

"Yeah, you just wanted to keep trying."

"Can you blame me?"

The kitchen door swung open, smacking a waitress with a full tray. The tray tipped and glasses wobbled, but she held onto it.

"I'm so sorry." Charles Sinclair, the door swinger, grabbed the heavy tray and steadied it. "Are you all right? Can I help?"

"I've got it, sir. Thank you." The waitress smiled at him.

Charles nodded and held the door for her. He looked around the kitchen and found what he wanted. "Where's my favorite girl?"

"Grandpa!" Charlotte squirmed out of her father's arms. "Grandpa's here!"

"Wow, did you just get ditched." Jack laughed as Charles hoisted the little girl into his arms.

"Oh yeah. She breaks my heart every time he comes over." Austin held his hand over his heart and pouted, but he couldn't hide the happy smile in his eyes. "I can't compete with Grandpa."

"That's because you don't bring her presents." Charles pulled a small doll from his pocket.

The little girl squealed and gave him a big sloppy kiss.

Charles studied the busy kitchen with a critical eye. "The place looks good, Jane. It took you long enough to pull this together. I can't believe you managed to do it."

She smiled, choosing to take that as a compliment. "Thank you, Charles."

"Jane...." The hostess stood in the kitchen doorway. "There's a woman here who says she wants to meet the chef."

"Wow. Already?" When she looked into the dining room, her smile froze.

Austin looked over her shoulder. "Do you want me to handle this? She likes me."

Jane rolled her eyes. "I still don't know how you managed that."

"It's a gift. She hasn't figured out how bad I really am."

"Come with me." She took his hand and led him out to the dining room. "Hi, Mom. I can't believe you came all the way out here to see this."

Gwen Elliot smiled at her daughter. "I wouldn't miss your opening night. I'm so proud of you, Jane."

Jane blinked back tears as her mother gave her an awkward hug.

"Hi, Mom." Austin wrapped his arms around Gwen. She stiffened for a moment, still not used to his enthusiastic affection. Then she relaxed and hugged him back.

"Hello, Austin, where's your sweet little angel?"

"She's got you fooled, doesn't she? She's in the kitchen charming grandpa."

"Of course."

"Come take a look, Mom." Jane led her mother and Charles on a guided tour.

Suddenly, the dining room got busy and Jane had to turn the entertaining duties over to her daughter while she took over the kitchen. Jack, Sara, and Austin offered to help, but Jane and her staff had everything under control.

Austin broke away from the family gathering and found her

stirring the soup. "My mom called. She said to tell you congratulations and she's sorry she couldn't make it tonight. She'll be here soon."

She nodded. "To tell you the truth, I'm kind of glad she isn't here."

"Because my dad is?"

"Uh-huh. I didn't want to deal with that drama again."

"Yeah. Our wedding was interesting enough to last me a few years."

Jane tasted the soup. It was very good but something was missing. "I wish my dad was here to see this."

"He would be so proud of you." Austin wrapped his arms around her and held her close. "I am."

"Thank you, Sweetheart."

Austin stood behind her while she added a little oregano to the soup. He wrapped his hands on her hips, nibbling her neck. "Mmm... you're the tastiest item on the menu."

She leaned back against him and sighed. "Keep tasting."

"Hey." He pressed his lips to her ear. "There's a guy right here who wants to see the chef... naked."

She laughed. "Well, Doctor, tell him if he can wait, he'll get a personal guided tour."

"That's what I like to hear." He glanced around the kitchen. "Have we christened the pantry yet?"

"That's next."

When the rush was over, the kitchen cleaned, and the staff sent home, Jane and Austin sat down with their friends and family for a meal she'd prepared especially for them.

"I would like to propose a toast." Jane raised her glass of wine.

Her guests followed suit, Gwen, Sara, and Jack raising their glasses of water. Charlotte looked around and raised her water glass too.

"To all of you here tonight—Sara, Jack, Charles, Mom, and especially Austin. It took a long time to get here—a lot of hard work, a lot of sleepless nights—but most of all, a lot of love and encouragement from you. I couldn't have done this on my own. I thank you all."

"Me too?" Charlotte giggled.

"You too, Sweetheart." Jane smiled. "Cheers."

"Cheers!"

About the Author

I got hooked on trashy romance novels in junior high, but my mom took them away from me. She couldn't stop me from daydreaming, though. After I got married, I wrote some of my naughtier daydreams down and sent them to *Playgirl* magazine. Two of them got published. I kept daydreaming and writing stories until my dirty stories turned into trashy books.

I live in Colorado, but I'll always be a loyal Wisconsin Cheesehead. When I'm not lusting after my next bad boy hero, I'm looking for inspiration in sci-fi and action movies, football players, morally ambiguous lawyers, muscle cars, and kick-butt chicks.

I'm known as "Trashy Writer" at various social media sites. I call myself a trashy writer because I want my readers to know that I enjoy mindless escapism as much as they do. I'm not out to win a Pulitzer Prize. (But I'm an award-winning finalist in erotica, USA Book News 2012.) I just want to help someone relax and get away from it all for a little while. I write romance, erotica and trash for fun and pleasure.

I hope you have as much fun reading it as I had writing it.

For more, please visit Amelia James online at:
Personal Website: http://trashytreasures.wordpress.com
Facebook: AuthorAmeliaJames
Goodreads: TrashyWriter
Google+: Amelia James
Twitter: TrashyWriter

What's Next from Amelia James?

THEIR TWISTED LOVE

Watch for this second installment in *The Twisted Mosaic* novels of erotica, coming May 21, 2013 from Evolved Publishing.

~~~~~~~~~~

Alex has everything he wants. He loves the power that comes with his job, and fooling around with his boss provides the illicit kink he needs. He's in charge and trusts no one.

Will should've learned something from his disastrous past, but he's distanced himself from everyone who loved him, keeping the pain in protective custody. He has no use for entanglements.

Talia has a new man, safe and secure—and boring as hell. She won't sleep with him until she knows she wants only him. But she can't forget, or forgive, the men who indulged her wildest fantasies and violated her trust.

They're happy apart... until Alex's case forces them back together, and Talia discovers she still craves both her former lovers. But only one loves her enough to satisfy her twisted desires and provide the stability she needs.

Sometimes, giving up control is the only way to keep it.
~~~~~~~~~~

Also by Amelia James:

SECRET STORM

This Contemporary Romance novel, featuring a return of the characters from *Tell Me You Want Me,* is now available.

~~~~~~~~~~

"I want to let you in, Jack, but I.... Oh hell, I just want you. I know you're not what I need, but I don't care. Take me to bed now and we'll sort the rest out later."

The last thing Sara Jensen needs is another risky relationship. She wants Jack, but she's been hurt too many times to trust him even though he's more than a friend. Jack won't trust her, and that hurts more than her ex's betrayal.

Jack Wheeler wants Sara. His long denied lust burns barely contained. But a dangerous secret comes back to haunt him, a secret so horrible he can't trust anyone with it, not even the woman he desires more than anything.

For the first time since they met, they're both available, but the timing couldn't be worse. Sara's not too eager to trust a man again, and Jack refuses to reveal his secret. Getting involved now is complicated, but Sara and Jack have waited long enough. Neither one of them can control their desires. But there's a storm approaching, and as hard as she tries, Sara can't run away from Jack's past. Jack won't accept her help, and Sara doesn't know how long she can wait for him to realize he needs her.
~~~~~~~~~~

Also by Amelia James:

HER TWISTED PLEASURES

This first installment in *The Twisted Mosaic* novels of erotica is now available.

~~~~~~~~~~~

His hand came off my neck and he wrapped his arms around me, crushing me against him. I grabbed his hair and forced his mouth to mine, feeding the darkness possessing us. Submission, yes! Not giving up control, but having it taken from me. This… this was why I needed Alex.

Will was too nice; he would never abuse me like this. But Alex…. Mmm… Alex had no such qualms. "What have you done to me?"

~~~

Talia indulges her sexual pleasures, turning her life into a twisted mess. Sleeping with Alex is dangerous and reckless. She craves that excitement. Loving Will is comforting and safe. She needs that stability. Why can't she get everything she wants from one man?

Will has everything under control, and watching his girlfriend flirt with his best friend fuels his lust for her. He loves Talia, and he trusts Alex. It's all good… as long as he makes the rules.

Alex doesn't give a damn about rules. He knows how to play with fire without getting burned. It's just *sex* with Talia. No emotions means no attachments—that's one rule he won't break.

Sometimes dirty little secrets are more dirty than secret.

Also by Amelia James:

THE DEVIL MADE ME DO IT

This collection of couples' erotica short stories is now available.

~~~~~~~~~~

"Don't tempt me."

Erin wants her husband to rip her clothes off... literally. Does she dare provoke him?

Natalie wants to make love outdoors. Can she convince her shy husband?

Melissa wants the bad boy she just met in a bar. Should she or shouldn't she?

And Heather watches from a secret room.

These women and others like them know what they want in bed. But sometimes they have to be a little extra bold to get it. Watch them bring their naughtiest fantasies to life in some very interesting ways.

"It wasn't my idea... the devil made me do it."
~~~~~~~~~~

Recommended Reading from Evolved Publishing:

CHILDREN'S PICTURE BOOKS

THE BIRD BRAIN BOOKS by Emlyn Chand:

Honey the Hero
Davey the Detective
Poppy the Proud
Tommy Goes Trick-or-Treating
Courtney Saves Christmas
Vicky Finds a Valentine

I'd Rather Be Riding My Bike by Eric Pinder
Valentina and the Haunted Mansion by Majanka Verstraete

HISTORICAL FICTION

Circles by Ruby Standing Deer
Spirals by Ruby Standing Deer
Stones by Ruby Standing Deer

LITERARY FICTION

Hannah's Voice by Robb Grindstaff
Jellicle Girl by Stevie Mikayne
Weight of Earth by Stevie Mikayne

LOWER GRADE

THE THREE LOST KIDS - SPECIAL EDITION ILLUSTRATED by Kimberly Kinrade:

Lexie World
Bella World
Maddie World

THE THREE LOST KIDS - CHAPTER BOOKS by Kimberly Kinrade:

The Death of the Sugar Fairy
The Christmas Curse
Cupid's Capture

MEMOIR

And Then It Rained: Lessons for Life by Megan Morrison

MYSTERY

Hot Sinatra by Axel Howerton

NEW ADULT
Desert Flower by Angela Scott
Desert Rice by Angela Scott
Torn Together by Emlyn Chand

ROMANCE / EROTICA
Melt My Heart by Darby Davenport
Skinny-Dipping at Dawn by Darby Davenport
Walk Away with Me by Darby Davenport
Her Twisted Pleasures by Amelia James
His Twisted Lesson by Amelia James
Secret Storm by Amelia James
Tell Me You Want Me by Amelia James
The Devil Made Me Do It by Amelia James
Their Twisted Love by Amelia James

SCI-FI / FANTASY
Eulogy by D.T. Conklin

SHORT STORY ANTHOLOGIES
FROM THE EDITORS AT EVOLVED PUBLISHING:
Evolution: Vol. 1 (A Short Story Collection)
Evolution: Vol. 2 (A Short Story Collection)
Pathways (A Young Adult Anthology)
All Tolkien No Action: Swords, Sorcery & Sci-Fi by Eric Pinder

SUSPENSE / THRILLER
Forgive Me, Alex by Lane Diamond
The Devil's Bane by Lane Diamond

YOUNG ADULT
Dead Embers by T.G. Ayer
Dead Radiance by T.G. Ayer
Farsighted by Emlyn Chand
Open Heart by Emlyn Chand
Pitch by Emlyn Chand
The Silver Sphere by Michael Dadich
Ring Binder by Ranee Dillon
Forbidden Mind by Kimberly Kinrade
Forbidden Fire by Kimberly Kinrade
Forbidden Life by Kimberly Kinrade
Forbidden Trilogy (Special Omnibus Edition) by Kimberly Kinrade
Survivor Roundup by Angela Scott
Wanted: Dead or Undead by Angela Scott

CPSIA information can be obtained at www.ICGtesting.com
Printed in the USA
LVOW10s1549130314

377222LV00016B/49/P